The Flick

Annie Baker

A Samuel French Acting Edition

SAMUEL FRENCH
FOUNDED 1830

SAMUELFRENCH.COM
SAMUELFRENCH-LONDON.CO.UK

FOR PRODUCTION ENQUIRIES

UNITED STATES AND CANADA
Info@SamuelFrench.com
1-866-598-8449

UNITED KINGDOM AND EUROPE
Plays@SamuelFrench-London.co.uk
020-7255-4302

Each title is subject to availability from Samuel French, depending
upon country of performance. Please be aware that *THE FLICK* may
not be licensed by Samuel French in your territory. Professional and
amateur producers should contact the nearest Samuel French office or
licensing partner to verify availability.

PRINTED IN CANADA

MUSIC USE NOTE

Licensees are solely responsible for obtaining formal written permission from copyright owners to use copyrighted music in the performance of this play and are strongly cautioned to do so. If no such permission is obtained by the licensee, then the licensee must use only original music that the licensee owns and controls. Licensees are solely responsible and liable for all music clearances and shall indemnify the copyright owners of the play(s) and their licensing agent, Samuel French, against any costs, expenses, losses and liabilities arising from the use of music by licensees. Please contact the appropriate music licensing authority in your territory for the rights to any incidental music.

IMPORTANT BILLING AND CREDIT REQUIREMENTS

If you have obtained performance rights to this title, please refer to your licensing agreement for important billing and credit requirements.

THE FLICK was first produced by Playwrights Horizons at the Mainstage Theatre in New York City on February 15, 2013. The performance was directed by Sam Gold, with sets and costumes by David Zinn, lighting by Jane Cox, and sound by Bray Poor. The Production Stage Manager was Katrina Herrmann. The cast was as follows:

SKYLAR/THE DREAMING MAN . . . . .Alex Hanna

ROSE . . . . Louisa Krause

SAM . . . . .Matthew Maher

AVERY . . . . Aaron Clifton Moten

CHARACTERS

SAM, 35 – shaved head. Caucasian. He often wears a beat-up Red Sox cap. He used to be very into Heavy Metal.

AVERY, 20 – African-American. bespectacled. He wears red, slightly European-looking sneakers. In love with the movies.

ROSE, 24 – Caucasian. sexually magnetic, despite the fact that (or partly because?) her clothes are baggy, she never wears makeup and her hair is dyed forest-green.

SKYLAR, 26/**THE DREAMING MAN**

SETTING

A falling-apart movie theater in Worcester County, MA. The set is the raked movie theater audience, ten to fifteen rows of red seats with a dingy carpeted aisle running up the center. The upstage wall is the back wall of the movie theater, with a window into the projection booth. There is a metal door leading out into the hallway to the movie theater lobby. We, the theater audience, are the movie screen. The beam of light from the projector radiates out over our heads.

TIME

Summer, 2012

A NOTE ON COSTUMES

Sam and Avery wear the same degrading movie theater uniform in every scene. It is a polo shirt (probably dark blue or purple or maroon) with a little name tag/pin, and black pants. Maybe the polo has "The Flick" embroidered in yellow or white on its chest pocket? Because Rose is the projectionist she doesn't have to wear a uniform. But maybe she wears the black pants anyway. Or the same pair of jeans every day.

"/" indicates where the next line of dialogue begins.

PRE-SHOW

After the theater audience has filed in, the house lights slowly dim (onstage in the movie audience and also in the theater audience). Bernard Herrmann's Prelude to "The Naked and the Dead"* starts playing, and the light from the projector beams out over our heads. Images that we cannot decipher are being projected. Dust motes are illuminated by the light.

This lasts 2 minutes (from beginning to end of the song) and all we can see are abstracted dancing images shooting out of the film projector.

Then the song ends, and the unknown movie ends, and there is a bright flash of green, and then white, and then the sound of the film reaching the end of its spool in the projector. The movie theater lights automatically flicker on, and after about 5 seconds...

---

* Please see Music Use Note on page 3

ACT ONE

Scene One

(The door at the back of the movie theater is thrown open.)

*(**SAM** peeks his head in, looks around, and then closes the door.)*

*(A second later, the door opens again and **SAM** drags in a large trash can that he uses to keep the door propped open. Then he exits again and re-enters carrying a push broom and dustpan. **AVERY** follows him in, carrying a push broom and dustpan of his own.)*

SAM. We call this the walkthrough.

(Pause.)

SAM. Pretty simple.

You just ah…

*(**AVERY** watches as **SAM** walks down the last row of seats with his broom, sweeping up popcorn kernels and trash and pushing them into the dustpan. When **SAM** finishes the last row and moves to the second-to-last row, **AVERY** awkwardly begins sweeping the last row on his side of the aisle. They continue this way, **SAM** always one row ahead of **AVERY**, each of them on his own side of the aisle. **AVERY** is trying to figure out the best way to sweep; it's harder than it looks. In the third-to-last row, **AVERY** encounters something we cannot see on the floor. He frowns with distaste, then bends over and gingerly picks up a Subway sandwich wrapper. Tiny pieces of shredded lettuce flutter to the ground. **SAM** looks over, stops what*

9

he's doing, and watches **AVERY**, *without offering any suggestions.)*

*(***AVERY*** *walks up the aisle, throws the Subway wrapper in the large trash can, along with the contents of his dust pan, then walks back and goes back to sweeping. For some reason it's not working—the tiny pieces of lettuce that we can't see are sticking to the ground.* **SAM** *is still watching him. After a while:)*

SAM. Yeah. With the little pieces of lettuce you kind of have to—

*(***AVERY*** *interrupts him by bending down to hand-pick the pieces of lettuce off the floor. He mostly disappears from view.)*

*(***SAM*** *watches, then goes back to sweeping. He's about three rows ahead of* **AVERY** *when* **AVERY** *finishes picking up the tiny pieces of lettuce. Cradling them in his palm,* **AVERY** *walks up the aisle again to the trash can and shakes his palm off into it. Then he goes back to sweeping. After moving on to the next aisle:)*

AVERY. What do you do about spilled soda?

SAM. We do one big mop at the end of the night.

*(***AVERY*** *nods. They go back to sweeping. After about twenty seconds:)*

AVERY. What if people are still here?

(A pause.)

SAM. Like—

AVERY. Have you ever had anyone like just sit here and refuse /to—

SAM. Sometimes people stay until the end of the credits. But then they go.

*(***AVERY*** *nods.)*

SAM. And they'll get the message when you start sweeping.

*(***AVERY*** *goes back to sweeping. After a pause:)*

SAM. Roberto told me that he once…that one time this couple was like having sex, like fully fucking on the seats when he came in.

AVERY. Whoa.

SAM. But he just like ignored them and like went about his business.

(They continue sweeping. After a pause:)

AVERY. Who's Roberto?

SAM. Oh. He doesn't work here anymore.

(Pause.)

SAM. He joined the Marines.

(Pause.)

AVERY. And who was the guy with the /big—

SAM. That was Brian.

Sundays and Mondays is Brian and Rebecca.

But you'll never meet them because you'll never work Sundays and Mondays.

(AVERY nods, a little uncomfortable. They go back to sweeping. They're almost done. SAM is in the second row and AVERY is in the fourth row.)

(When SAM finishes he just watches AVERY.)

SAM. Did Steve tell you about the soda machines?

AVERY. Uh…like…

SAM. How to clean them? About the seltzer?

AVERY. …No…

SAM. You gotta soak the spouts in seltzer overnight.

AVERY. Oh. Okay. Cool.

SAM. I'll show you.

In a minute.

(About ten more seconds, then AVERY finishes sweeping. They head up the aisle together, and dump their dustpans in the trash can. Then SAM takes the trash can

*and starts rolling it out the door. They are almost out the
door when* **SAM** *says:*)

SAM. So you're into movies?

AVERY. What? I mean yeah! I love movies.

(*And they're gone. The door swings shut behind them.
Blackout.*)

Scene Two

(SAM, alone in the middle of the theater, sweeping. After a few seconds, AVERY runs in, fastening his little pin and holding his broom.)

AVERY. Hey!

SAM. Hi Avery.

(Pause.)

AVERY. Sorry / I'm—

SAM. You're late.

AVERY. Yeah. I was just about to…yeah. I'm really sorry.

SAM. Yeah. Uh-huh. I /just—

AVERY. My dad was supposed to give me a ride but then he couldn't and I had to take like three different buses to get here and I'm still trying to figure /out the whole—

SAM. Uh-huh, yeah, I don't really need an explana/tion, it's just—

AVERY. No, no, of course, I just feel bad and I can totally reassure you that it won't happen again.

(Pause.)

SAM. It just puts me in an awkward position because /I'm—

AVERY. The thing is, I'm actually like…I'm actually like this obsessively punctual person and I'm like never ever late and this was just like a crazy um anomaly with the buses and now I know and I can promise you it will never happen again.

(Pause.)

SAM. Fine. Fine.

(Pause. SAM goes back to sweeping, then:)

SAM. I mean, it's no big deal.

But I'm sort of defacto in charge on Saturdays/and—

AVERY. No, I know.

SAM. It just puts me in an awkward position. That's all. Steve's never here so it was it was just me and I /had to—

AVERY. I can promise you that it won't happen again.

(Pause.)

SAM. I had to do soda and make a whole batch of popcorn by /myself.

AVERY. I'm so sorry.

SAM. No. It's cool.

(Pause. They both start sweeping. Then, unable to help himself:)

SAM. I'm just like—I don't know why Steve doesn't fucking promote me. I'm so sick of this shit.

*(**AVERY** nods, a little confused.)*

SAM. I should be a fucking projectionist by now!

AVERY. Oh. Yeah. I'd love to do that.

SAM. Well, he'll probably promote you before he promotes me. He like clearly thinks I'm *diseased* or something.
(Pause.)

SAM. He promoted Rose and I've worked here five months longer than her.

(They go back to sweeping.)

SAM. *(looking down at the floor in his row)* Aw fuck.

What is this?

*(**AVERY** stops and peers over from his side of the aisle.)*

SAM. Someone spilled like chocolate pudding or something. Are you fucking kidding me?

AVERY. Are you sure it's not, like…shit?

*(A pause. **SAM** bends down and inspects it.)*

AVERY. Oh god.

SAM. …Definitely not shit.

AVERY. Are you sure?

SAM. Uh-huh.

AVERY. Because I'm kind of um...I'm kind of shit-phobic.

SAM. There are like weird little *balls* in it.

It's like *chocolate tapioca pudding.*

Who brings pudding into a movie theater??!!

*(**SAM** gazes at it for a while, then straightens up, steps around it, and goes back to sweeping. **SAM** notices **AVERY** watching him and gets a little self-conscious.)*

SAM. ...I'll take care of it later.

(They sweep for a while. Then:)

SAM. What does that mean, shit-phobic?

AVERY. Like other people's shit makes me like...it like makes me want to puke.

SAM. Well sure.

AVERY. Yeah. But with me it's like really...like if I go into the stall and someone has, um, like if someone's left something there I actually sometimes like...I actually need to puke.

Like sometimes I actually puke.

SAM. Huh.

(Pause.)

SAM. Have you heard of that website where people send in pictures of their shit and then other people rate it?

AVERY. Yes I have heard of that website. That website is like my worst nightmare.

*(**SAM** giggles.)*

SAM. So if I wanted to be really like cruel I could like leave my laptop open with that website up and you /would—

AVERY. I would literally puke all over your laptop.

*(**SAM** giggles.)*

SAM. Oh man.

(*A happy pause in which they realize they've broken the
tension, and then awkward pause following that happy
pause. They go back to sweeping. A minute later, someone
appears in the window of the projection booth. It is a
girl. She is moving around, changing film, appearing in
and out of view.*)

(**SAM** *notices her.*)

SAM. Oh. Hey. That's Rose.

(**AVERY** *looks up.*)

SAM. HEY ROSE!

(*She doesn't hear him. After a little while:*)

SAM. Huh.

I guess she like hates me or something.

ROSE!

(*pause*)

ROSE!!

Wow.

She really hates me.

AVERY. Maybe she can't hear you.

SAM. She can hear me.

Rose!

I want to introduce you to her. She's cool.

ROSE!!!!!!!!!

(**ROSE** *continues moving around in the projection booth,
oblivious.*)

SAM. (*a cry of pure agony/unrequited love*) ROOOOSSSSSE!!!!!!!

(**ROSE** *remains oblivious.*)

SAM. Well.

She officially hates me.

(**SAM** *and* **AVERY** *gaze up the projection booth while* **ROSE** *moves around, then disappears from view.* **AVERY** *goes back to sweeping.* **SAM** *keeps watching the window as if he hopes she might appear again. This goes on for about ten seconds, then:*)

(*Blackout.*)

Scene Three

*(A few days later. **SAM** and **AVERY** are in the middle of sweeping, on their separate sides of the aisle.)*

SAM. Jack Nicholson.

Jack Nicholson and uh…

And uh…

Renée—no.

Dakota Fanning.

Jack Nicholson and Dakota Fanning.

(A short pause.)

AVERY. That's too easy.

SAM. Well just do it then.

AVERY. …Jack Nicholson to Tom Cruise in *A Few Good Men.*

Tom Cruise to Dakota Fanning in *War of the Worlds.*

SAM. Huh.

AVERY. Come up with a better one.

SAM. Fine. Fine.

Uh….

Pauly Shore.

Pauly Shore and uh…

Ian Holm.

AVERY. Okay.

*(**AVERY** thinks. He squints and raises his index finger, as if drawing complicated algebraic equations in the air. After about six seconds…)*

AVERY. Pauly Shore to Stephen Baldwin in *Biodome.*

SAM. You have it already?

AVERY. Stephen Baldwin to Kevin Pollack in *The Usual Suspects.*

Uh…uh…Kevin Pollack to Bruce Willis in…uh…let's say…*The Whole Nine Yards.*

SAM. What do you mean "let's say"?

AVERY. They were also in *The Whole Ten Yards* together and—I think—*Hostage*.

And then Bruce Willis to Ian Holm in *The Fifth Element.*

SAM. Jesus.

AVERY. Make it harder.

SAM. Uh…uh…uh…

Uh…

Michael J Fox! Michael J Fox and uh…

Ooh. Okay.

Michael J Fox and Britney Spears.

(AVERY nods.)

AVERY. Okay.

(He closes his eyes. About ten seconds pass.)

SAM. Ooh-hooh. This one is hard.

(AVERY's mouth moves slightly and his eyes do strange things as he does his calculations.)

SAM. This is a doozie.

(AVERY's eyebrows raise—it seems like he is getting somewhere—but then he clearly reaches a roadblock.)

SAM. Ooooo boy.

Uh-oh.

(About twenty more seconds of silent calculation. Eventually AVERY unties some kind of complicated mental knot, opens his eyes, and grins.)

SAM. No.

NO!

AVERY. This one takes a full six degrees but I'm happy with it.

(pause)

Britney to Kim Cattrall in *Crossroads.*

SAM. Okay.

AVERY. Kim Cattrall to Estelle Geddy in *Mannequin*.

SAM. *Mannequin*!

My first sexual fantasy EVER was about Kim Cattrall in *Mannequin*!

AVERY. I've actually never seen it.

SAM. It's the best. It's the best. Cattrall is this mannequin who comes to life and Andrew McCarthy is the department store worker window guy who falls in love with her. And Estelle Geddy is the store manager.

I don't remember *why* exactly Kim Cattrall comes to life. There's some sort of magic Egyptian-y reason behind it. And then she/like—

AVERY. Estelle Geddy to Sylvester Stallone in *Stop Or My Mom Will Shoot*.

Sylvester Stallone to John Lithgow in Cliffhanger.

Lithgow to Christopher Lloyd in…uh…okay…I'm pretty sure this is the title: "Adventures of Buckaroo Bonsai Across the Eighth Dim/ension."

SAM. WHOA!!

WHAT THE FUCK!!!

YES!!

I LOVE THAT MOVIE!

AVERY. Christopher Lloyd to Michael J Fox in, of course…

SAM. *Back to the Future.*   **AVERY**. *Back to the Future.*
Parts One through
Three.

(*A pause.* **SAM** *stares at* **AVERY**, *in awe. They don't notice* **ROSE** *enter the projection booth.*)

SAM. You have like a…that's like almost like a *disability*.

AVERY. It's actually like the opposite of a disability.

(**ROSE** *knocks on the window of the projection booth and waves at them.*)

SAM. Oh! Jesus!

    *(to **AVERY**)*

    That's Rose.

AVERY. I know.

    *(They wave back. **ROSE** breathes on the window, making a little foggy area, and then draws a cartoon penis in the fog with her finger. It may or may not be decipherable.)*

AVERY. What is that.

SAM. …I *think* it's a penis.

    *(**ROSE** draws a heart around the penis.)*

AVERY. Whoa.

SAM. Yeah.

    She's a lesbian.

AVERY. Really?

SAM. Yep.

    *(**ROSE** is unthreading the projector now, mostly obscured from view.)*

AVERY. Does she have a girlfriend?

SAM. Shhh. Uh. No. I don't think so.

    *(They go back to sweeping. They don't see **ROSE** leave the projection booth. They keep sweeping. **ROSE** appears in the doorway. She regards **SAM** and **AVERY**, then:)*

ROSE. Hi. I'm Rose.

AVERY. I'm Avery.

AVERY. Yeah.   **ROSE**. Avery, right?

    (Pause.)

ROSE. How old are you?

AVERY. 20.

ROSE. Huh.

    (Pause.)

ROSE. I like your shoes.

    *(**AVERY** looks down at his shoes.)*

ROSE. Red.

 (Pause.)

AVERY. …Thanks.

 (Another pause.)

ROSE. Hi Sam.

SAM. Hello Rose.

 (Pause.)

ROSE. I'm really hungover so you guys will have to excuse me if I'm like a little low-energy tonight.

 *(**AVERY** goes back to cleaning. **ROSE** leans sleepily against the wall. **SAM** seems eager to talk to her.)*

SAM. Who were you out with?

ROSE. *(fake-spaced-out)* What?

SAM. Oh. Uh. Who were you partying with last night?

ROSE. Just a couple of friends.

SAM. Katie?

ROSE. Oh my god. Katie is like…no.

 Reiko. And this other guy.

 We all drank moonshine…have you guys ever had moonshine?

SAM. Uh-huh.   **AVERY**. No.

ROSE. Anyway. I'm just like…I totally have a drinking problem.

 *(She fake yawns. **AVERY** accidentally drops his broom, then quickly picks it up.)*

 I'm gonna go take a nap. When does the next show start?

SAM. 6:20.

 Do you need anything? I could like run out and get you something.

ROSE. Oh my god no. I'm totally fine.

(She starts to leave, then stops)

ROSE. It was nice meeting you Avery.

AVERY. Yeah. You too.

ROSE. Those shoes rock.

(ROSE exits. SAM stands there. AVERY continues sweeping. After a safe amount of time has gone by:)

SAM. ...So?

AVERY. What?

SAM. What'd you think?

AVERY. She was—

(ROSE reenters.)

ROSE. *(to SAM)* Did you tell him about dinner money?

(SAM gets weird.)

SAM. Uh—what? No. Wait—

ROSE. What did you do last night?
Did you take it all?

SAM. I thought that—he just started working here, /so—

ROSE. Well. Exactly, dumbass. You have to explain it to him.

SAM. It's just—we have no idea if he's going to be cool with /it and—

ROSE. He *has* to be cool with it.

(AVERY is trying to look like he's not listening.)

SAM. Hey. Avery.

(AVERY turns around.)

AVERY. Yeah.

SAM. At the end of every shift you're gonna get Dinner Money. It's just a little extra cash. We always split it three ways or two ways if there's just two of us. It can be anywhere from you know ten bucks on a weeknight to like thirty bucks on the weekend.

AVERY. Oh. Cool.

(Short pause.)

ROSE. *(to* **SAM***)* See? It's fine.   **AVERY.** So it's like a *per diem?*

ROSE. A what?

SAM. No. Uh. Well. Kind of. It's kind of like a *per diem.* It's just…

Steve doesn't know about it.

(A weird pause.)

AVERY. Steve doesn't give it to us?

*(***ROSE*** looks at* **SAM***.* **SAM*** struggles to find the right way to say it.)*

SAM. When we…when we take the tickets, we just kind of…you know when you tear them in half and put the other half in the/bin, well—

AVERY. Yeah. Sure.

SAM. Well, sometimes we take like, uh, like 10 percent of those stubs, and we, uh, we, uh, we, uh, resell them.

(A pause.)

SAM. And then we take 10 percent of the, uh, the, uh… cash for the night.

ROSE. As dinner money.

SAM. We call it dinner money.

ROSE. Well, it *is* kind of dinner money, because we're so vastly underpaid and because Steve is a total douchebag and doesn't have a credit card machine and is like totally fishy anyway with his finances and basically has like no idea how to run a movie theater.

(A pause.)

ROSE. So actually it like, it *is* dinner money.

Because 8.25 an hour is *not* enough to live on.

AVERY. You've never been caught?

ROSE. No, it's like a like a like an employee tradition? Roberto—the guy who trained me—he told me about it and the people who worked here before him told *him* about it and like nobody has ever been caught or like even been close to being caught.

Because Steve is just like...he's an idiot.

He can like suck my cock.

(AVERY looks at SAM. SAM is embarrassed.)

AVERY. Uh...so what are you guys asking me?

ROSE. I guess we're not asking you anything.	**AVERY**. Because I don't really want to do it.
ROSE. But you can't... it's not up to you to decide!	**SAM**. You don't have to do anything! I'll deal with the tickets! You just get half the money!

AVERY. I don't want to take Steve's money.

ROSE. Okay, see, I don't think of it as Steve's money. Steve is like a compulsive gambler who doesn't pay child support. He has like five kids somewhere in like Maine and his ex-wife is always taking him to court.

(A long pause.)

AVERY. I don't want the money. I'm not gonna like rat you guys out but, no, I'm sorry, I could tell he didn't really want to hire a black guy anyway and/I'm not gonna—

SAM. WHOA! Really?! Steve is a racist?!!

AVERY. I don't know, okay? That's/what I'm—

ROSE. That's so lame. That's so lame. He's such a fucking racist.

AVERY. I'm not saying...I'm just...he's like an older angry white dude with a truck and like...it's just one of those things...where like if something goes wrong...

(A very long, uncomfortable pause.)

ROSE. *I* don't feel that way.

(Pause.)

AVERY. Wait, what?

(Another weird pause.)

SAM. Can I just say...I guess I just want to say that, uh, Roberto...Roberto was Hispa—Latino?

And uh nothing ever happened.

Nothing bad ever happened to him.

*(Silence. **AVERY** walks down the aisle, sits in the front row of the theater, and puts his head in his hands. They watch him.)*

(After a second, he takes off his glasses, wipes them off on his polo, puts them back on, and then puts his head in his hands again.)

*(**SAM** and **ROSE** watch him do this, and then start mouthing panicky silent things to each other. Maybe **ROSE** is mouthing stuff like WHAT DO WE DO??!! HE'S GONNA TELL ON US!! and **SAM** is mouthing stuff like IT'S COOL IT'S COOL I'LL TALK TO HIM IT'S GONNA BE COOL but we shouldn't really be able to read their lips and maybe they can't either, it's more just like mutual gestures of panic.)*

*(Then they go back to watching **AVERY**, who is unmoving in his seat.)*

SAM. If you have like—

If it's like an ethical you know—

You could always uh...

(He trails off. Another silence.)

ROSE. Listen.

Avery.

I don't want to be like a total cunt about this and I don't want to put you in a crappy position.

But if me and Sam are doing it and you're not it's like...it's like not fair to anybody. Like it's like really bad for everyone involved.

*(A few seconds later, **AVERY** stands up, shakes his head as if to clear it, puts his hands on his hips.)*

AVERY. Yeah.

Okay.

Fine.

(Pause.)

ROSE. Wait, what does /that—

AVERY. It's fine.

I'll take—I'll do whatever.

It's cool.

Sorry.

I didn't mean to like…

I didn't mean to freak you guys out.

Or be judgmental.

(pause)

Sorry. Yeah.

I'm okay with it.

(They stare at him.)

(He laughs nervously.)

AVERY. Seriously!!

I'm fine.

Sorry.

*(**ROSE** and **SAM** exchange a long look. Then:)*

ROSE. …All right, boys.

I'm gonna go take a nap in the booth.

Wake me up at five till.

*(She leaves. **SAM** looks at **AVERY**. **AVERY** finally stands up. They resume sweeping. After a little while:)*

SAM. Richard Pryor and Angelina Jolie.

(Blackout.)

Scene Four

(**SAM** *and* **AVERY** *are in the middle of sweeping.* **AVERY** *is whistling to himself ("Le Tourbillon" from "Jules and Jim"). After about a minute:*)

SAM. You know what I hate the most?

(**AVERY** *stops whistling.*)

SAM. It's one thing if I sold you the food. It's one thing if you, you know, legitimately purchased the food from me and then leave it like scattered across the floor.

But to SNEAK FOOD IN...

To sneak outside food in and THEN to like scatter it across the floor and leave empty bags of...

(*he lifts up the bag*)

...Sun Chips on your seat.

That I do not understand.

AVERY. I feel the opposite.

SAM. What do you mean?

AVERY. It feels so weird when I sold it to them. It's like, I gave you that popcorn. I like scooped it out myself and put it in the bag and handed it to you and you paid me and said thank you.

And now it's all over the floor.

SAM. Huh.

AVERY. With the Sun Chips it's like...it's just regular litter.

SAM. Interesting.

Interesting perspective.

(*They continue sweeping.* **AVERY** *resumes his whistling.*)

(*After a while:*)

SAM. (*incredulous*) Someone left a shoe.

(*He lifts a shoe up in the air disdainfully.*)

SAM. Someone left a nasty nasty old New Balance shoe.

AVERY. Do you think it was intentional?

SAM. Like is it a sign of gang *warfare* or something?

AVERY. No. Like do you think someone forgot it and left here with one shoe on…

Or do you think they like meant to throw it away?

(a short pause)

Like do we put it in the lost and found?

SAM. Fuck no.

Fuck no.

It smells disgusting.

*(**SAM** walks up the aisle to the trash can, holding the shoe by its lace.)*

SAM. Uch. Uch. Uch. Uch.

UchUchUchUchUchUchUch.

(He throws the shoe in the trash.)

*(Then **SAM** reaches under his polo and scratches his collarbone.)*

SAM. My *neck* itches.

(They continue sweeping. After about twenty seconds:)

AVERY. Hey.

What do you wanna, like…

What do you wanna like be when you grow up?

(Pause.)

SAM. …I am grown up.

AVERY. Oh.

Yeah. I guess I just mean /like—

SAM. That's like the most depressing thing anyone's ever said to me.

AVERY. Sorry.

(They finish sweeping. They dump their dustpans into the trash.)

(On their way out the door:)

SAM. A chef.

(Blackout.)

Scene Five

(Darkness. The final credits of a movie. Swelling music. Light from the projector.)

*(A **DREAMING MAN** has stayed till the end of the credits.)*

*(The music ends. A flash of green. A flash of white. The lights in the theater automatically flicker on. A few seconds later, **AVERY** and **SAM** come in through the door, in the middle of a conversation. This time they have mops and a large yellow mop bucket on wheels. It is the end of the night.)*

SAM. *(not noticing there is still someone in the theater)* I disagree. I *strongly* disagree.

AVERY. Name one. Name one great American movie made in the—

*(**AVERY** notices the Dreaming Man and stops talking.)*

(The man is in the fifth or sixth row, lightly sleeping, facing forward. Maybe his head is subtly listing to one side as he sleeps.)

*(**SAM** and **AVERY** start to clean, waiting for him to go. The man is on **AVERY**'s side of the aisle. **AVERY** eventually walks over, looks at the man, and sees that he's asleep.)*

*(**AVERY** isn't sure what to do. He gesticulates for **SAM** to come over. **SAM** comes over.)*

AVERY. *(to the man)* Excuse me.

(The man doesn't move or wake up.)

*(**SAM** pokes his shoulder, a little too aggressively.)*

(The man jolts awake and stares at them.)

SAM. The movie is over.

THE DREAMING MAN. Oh. Sorry.

(**SAM** *walks back to his side of the theater and resumes cleaning.* **AVERY** *remains standing in the aisle, holding his mop, unsure of what to do. The man wipes the sleep from his eyes, maybe searches for something on the floor, gathers his things, and then departs, not making eye contact. He walks up the aisle, head bowed, and out the door. It slams behind him.*)

(*A pause, then:*)

SAM. *Avatar!* *Avatar* was a great movie made in the last ten years.

AVERY. I…what?!

(*More incredulous pausing.*)

AVERY. Okay. Uh. If you think that, if you actually think that, I can't even like…I can't even like continue to have this conversation.

If you actually think that I need to like quit this job.

SAM. *Avatar* was a great movie.

(*Pause.*)

Avatar was a work of genius!

AVERY. I can't even…I can't even…

Words are failing me.

SAM. Oh so like oh so you think you're like *better* than *Avatar*. Like you're above *Avatar*.

AVERY. No. I/just—

SAM. Because I bet you really fucking enjoyed *Avatar*. I bet you had a blast at *Avatar*. And now you're like looking down your nose at *Avatar* because it didn't have like German subtitles or whatever.

AVERY. I repeat: I don't think it's possible for me to engage in like a rational debate with you about it.

SAM. Oh come on.

AVERY. It's like if I said: I love killing babies. Let me like try to convince you why killing babies is fun and you should enjoy killing babies.

*(They go back to mopping. Unnoticed by them, **ROSE** appears in the projection booth, cleaning up, unwinding the film.)*

(Silence for a while, then finally, unable to help himself:)

AVERY. It was a video game.

SAM. Excuse me?

AVERY. *Avatar* was basically like a video game.

SAM. It was not a video game.

A video game is interactive.

A video game is defined by the fact that you're…that you're…

(moving on)

It was 3-D. That was fucking awesome. Did you see it in 3-D?

AVERY. Uh-huh.

SAM. It's just like different and that like scares you. People always freak out when like you know when like art forms move forward.

AVERY. That's not the art form moving forward. That's the art form moving backwards. 3-D was around in like the 50s.

*(**ROSE** leaves the projection booth.)*

SAM. I thought it was totally awesome-looking.

AVERY. I don't like digital. Period.

SAM. It's where film is going.

AVERY. Well then it won't be film anymore. It'll be computer-generated crap.

*(**ROSE** enters, holding a book.)*

ROSE. Hey. Look what I found on the street.

*(**SAM** walks over to her and reads the title out loud:)*

SAM. "Astrology and Your Love Life: How to Find True Compatibility and Long Lasting Relationships."

ROSE. What's your sign?

SAM. Uh...Leo.

ROSE. Oh my god me too.

(**ROSE** *flips through the book.*)

ROSE. What about you, Avery?

(*After a short pause:*)

AVERY. I don't know.

ROSE. Excuse me?

AVERY. I don't remember.

I don't really care about that kind of thing.

ROSE. Oh my god. Oh my god.

You are so full of shit!

AVERY. I don't believe in astrology.

ROSE. Okay, that's fine, but you know what your sign is. I don't buy for a second that you don't know what your sign is.

(*Pause.*)

ROSE. Oh my god, Avery!

Don't even try to *pretend* with me that you don't know what /your—

AVERY. Capricorn.

ROSE. ...Thank you.

(*She flips through the book again.*)

SAM. Hey Rose.

ROSE. (*still looking through the book*) Ye-es...

SAM. Avery thinks there hasn't been a single great movie made in the past ten years.

AVERY. Single great *American* movie.

ROSE. (*still flipping*) Uh-huh.

SAM. And I think he's wrong.

AVERY. (*to* **SAM**) *Pulp Fiction* was the last *truly* great American movie and that was '94.

SAM. You have to do some of it for Rose.

AVERY. No.

ROSE. Do what?

SAM. He has like all of *Pulp Fiction* memorized and he can/ like—

AVERY. Nope.

SAM. Do Ezekiel 25:17!

AVERY. No way.

SAM. *(to* **ROSE***)* He does the most like incredible Samuel L. Jackson imitation.

"THE PATH OF THE RIGHTEOUS BROTHER IS BESET ON ALL SIDES BY THE TYRANNY OF THE WEAK"!

*(***ROSE*** eyes ***AVERY*** dubiously.)*

AVERY. That's not how it goes.

(A pause.)

ROSE. What about *Million Dollar Baby*?

AVERY. What about it?

ROSE. That's a great movie.

AVERY. That is not a great movie.

SAM. Avery is like a film snob.

ROSE. *Tree of Life*?

*(A grim silence. ***SAM*** shakes his head, embarrassed.)*

ROSE. Oh boy. You both hate *Tree of Life*.

Okay.

Sam and Avery, I'm gonna read you your compatibility.

It's me and Avery's compatibility too because I'm also a Leo.

SAM. *Magnolia*!

There Will Be Blood.

AVERY. Those are good movies. Very good movies.

But ultimately disappointing.

SAM. *Lord of the Rings*! *Return of the King*!

AVERY. Are you kidding me?

SAM. Uh uh uh uh…

The third Bourne movie!

The Bourne Ultimatum!

AVERY. This is a pointless debate.

SAM. Oh come on!

Those Bourne movies are like like like fine wines!

(**AVERY** *shakes his head.*)

Uh…*The Aviator!* Wait. Never mind.

ROSE. *(reading loudly)* "Leo and Capricorn."

"It's hard to make this combination of personalities work in a long-term love relationship."

Ooh. Sorry guys.

SAM. *(rolling his eyes)* Ha ha.

ROSE. "Orderly and organized Capricorn is likely to disapprove of Leo's exuberance and spontaneity. Leo has a bad temper but is quick to forgive and forget; Capricorn is more even-tempered but can hold a grudge for years. Capricorn is also the more devoted partner and Leos tend to have a wandering eye. Most of all, Capricorn and Leo are not sexually compatible. They are both dominators and yet almost complete opposites. Prudent practical Capricorn is often a bit of a snob and fairly /conservative—

SAM. OH MY GOD! I JUST SAID HE WAS A SNOB!

AVERY I JUST CALLED YOU A SNOB!

AVERY. Uh-huh.

ROSE. "…often a bit of a snob and fairly conservative, and will probably try to tamp down Leo's adventurous and impetuous personality."

Uh…what else…blah blah blah…

"Capricorn is an Earth sign and Leo is a fire sign…it can take Capricorn a while to open up his/her heart but once Capricorn opens it he/she is extremely loyal…but it will be very hard to make this marriage work…"

Ooh!

Wait. There's a "Business and Career section"!

AVERY. That's probably more relevant.

ROSE. "Business and Career."

Hey!

"The career connection between Leo and Capricorn is fantastic"!

"They are both excited to learn from one another. Usually one partner has more experience and will *show the other the ropes.*"

(She looks up and grins.)

SAM. …Whoa.

That's weird.

That's…Actually Weird.

ROSE. "As long as there is not a power struggle there can be an incredible and fruitful collaboration."

Uh…

"Connections with the arts are favored"!

SAM. No!!

(He looks over her shoulder.)

SAM. *(to* **AVERY***)* It actually says that!!

ROSE. *(shutting the book)* That is awesome, you guys.

*(***SAM** *stands there, stunned.)*

SAM. So weird.

So weird.

(pause)

I mean I don't believe in that stuff but that is SO WEIRD.

*(***AVERY** *goes back to mopping.)*

SAM. You don't think that's weird??!!

ROSE. He's just being a typical Capricorn.

SAM. Ha ha! Yes! Prudent and practical!

(**AVERY** *cracks a smile.*)

SAM. *(to* **ROSE***, summoning up the courage)* What about us?

ROSE. What about us?

SAM. Leo on Leo.

I mean, Leo with Leo.

ROSE. Oh.

(*She flips through the book nonchalantly.*)

Hmmm…I think the same sign together is usually a bad thing…let's see…

"Leo and Leo."

"When this relationship is good it is very good, but when it is bad it is terrible. Leos have a very strong sex drive, so this couple will be highly compatible in bed. This is a kinky, passionate connection, but can sometimes be hard to sustain in a long-term way. These two Leos are king and queen of the jungle. It will either be a great love or a great rivalry. The big question is: who's the boss? There will be heartfelt embraces but also egos butting heads. Compromise is key in the fiery relationship between two Leos."

(*Pause.* **SAM** *is blushing.*)

SAM. *(trying to sound unimpressed)* Huh.

(**ROSE** *closes the book.*)

ROSE. I wonder what sign Reiko is.

SAM. What's our career connection?

ROSE. Yeah. I'm bored.

(*She gets up.*)

ROSE. *(to* **AVERY***)* See ya later, Capricorn.

AVERY. Uh-huh.

(*She leaves.*)

SAM. Wes Anderson.

Rushmore.

AVERY. That was '98.

And that is a good movie, but not a *Pulp Fiction* level good movie.

(They mop for a while.)

SAM. I think he has a new one coming out this winter.

(short pause)

Tarantino.

AVERY. *Django Unchained.*

SAM. What?

AVERY. It's called *Django Unchained.*

(More mopping.)

SAM. The Coen Brothers!

All the Coen Brothers movies.

No Country for Old Men.

*A Single...*what's it called.

AVERY. *A Serious Man.*

SAM. *Fargo*!! *Fargo.*

AVERY. First of all, *Fargo* was '96.

Second of all, those are all pretty good movies. Those are *interesting* movies.

But those are not like like like like...profound commentaries on /like—

SAM. Do you find Rose attractive?

(Pause.)

AVERY. Wait—do I find—

Rose?

SAM. Yes. Rose.

I feel like you guys have kind of a flirty antagonistic banter thing going on.

AVERY. I mean uh—I don't know. No. Not really.

SAM. Not *really*?

AVERY. No. I mean no.

She's…she kind of makes me uncomfortable.

SAM. …Huh.

AVERY. She's a lesbian anyway, so/it—

SAM. Yeah.

Yeah.

AVERY. Do *you* find Rose/attr—

SAM. Shhhhhhh.

(They clean for a while.)

SAM. Hey. Will you come over here and look at my neck?

(AVERY puts down his mop and walks over to SAM.)

SAM. Does it look weird?

AVERY. Well there are all these red blotches but I can't tell if that's because you've been scratching it.

SAM. What about my back?

My back itches too.

(SAM turns around and lifts up the bottom of his shirt.)

AVERY. Oh. Yeah.

SAM. Yeah what?

AVERY. Yeah. There are a bunch of red like…

They're like little red lesions or something.

SAM. Lesions??

AVERY. Like they're kind of red oval shaped…

Auggh!

(AVERY pulls SAM's shirt down.)

SAM. What? What?

AVERY. They started freaking me out.

SAM. Great.

Fucking great.

I'm gonna go look in the bathroom.

*(**SAM** exits. **AVERY** keeps mopping, by himself. He reaches the front row. **ROSE** knocks on the window of the projection booth. **AVERY** looks up. **ROSE** smiles and mouths something he (and we) can't understand.)*

AVERY. What?

(She mouths it again.)

AVERY. Wait, what?

*(She flaps her hand in the air, as if to say "forget about it," and then goes back to dethreading the projector. **AVERY** continues mopping.)*

*(**SAM** walks back in.)*

SAM. Weird.

Some of them are like *scaly*.

What the fuck.

AVERY. Have you ever had chickenpox?

SAM. Yeah. Twice.

When I was a kid.

It's definitely not chickenpox.

(A pause.)

SAM. ...Repulsive.

*(**AVERY** doesn't really know how to respond to this so he finishes mopping his first row and then moves on to **SAM**'s side and keeps mopping. **SAM** just stands there.)*

(Blackout.)

Scene Six

(**AVERY**, *alone in the theater, squatting on the back
of one of the seats, talking to his therapist on his cell
phone.*)

AVERY. Yeah.

Well.

How do you like *do* that? How do you like ask someone
to be friends with—

(*A long pause.*)

AVERY. Uh-huh.

And…

Yeah.

Well that makes me feel insecure too.

(*Pause.*)

AVERY. Oh!

I finally remembered one of my dreams.

(*pause*)

Yeah.

(*smiling*)

I *thought* you'd be happy about that.

(*pause, glancing at the door*)

We're on a break.

Everyone went to Subway.

(*pause*)

Okay. So in the dream I'm dead. I mean, I've just died.
And I'm in this weird room. Which is basically like
purgatory. And there's a whole bunch of us, a bunch
of people who just died, and we're all waiting to see
if we can, you know, move on. To the next level. Oh.
And my dad is there. Because he just died too. And
then the room suddenly turns into my dad's study. And

this person starts scanning all the books on my dad's bookshelves with this ISBN-type scanner thing and they run the scanner over all of his books and eventually one of the books goes like BEEP BEEP BEEP and the scanner recognizes it and that means my dad is going on to heaven.

And then it's my turn.

(*pause*)

Um. Wait. Sorry.

Are you bored?

I just got scared you were bored again.

Like I don't know how you could possibly be interested in this.

(*pause*)

Because that doesn't make sense to me.

(*pause*)

Uh-huh.

(*pause*)

Okay.

Um.

So I'm up next. And suddenly I'm surrounded by all these shelves and on every shelf is every movie I've ever seen. And like some are like DVDs and other are like old VHS tapes from like the '90s and some are even like old 35 millimeter reels, like movies I saw in the theater. And like—yeah. Everything is there. Like *The Wizard of Oz*, which is the first movie I ever saw. And like old Jim Carrey movies and the entire Criterion Collection...and then they hand me the ISBN scanner and I realize, like, I realize that the way they decide whether or not you get into heaven is through, like, looking at all the movies you've ever watched or all the books you've ever read and figuring out whether there was one book or movie that you truly truly loved. Like one movie that like symbolizes your entire life.

And I think, okay, I'm gonna be fine. I love movies and I've seen all these like awesome movies, this is gonna be no problem, and I start running the scanner across the shelves. I run it across all these Kung Fu movies I watched in high school, I run it across all of Truffaut's movies, and the scanner isn't beeping. It's weird. It's not recognizing anything. And then I run it over *Pierrot Le Fou* and *Barry Lyndon*, and I've seen those movies like literally dozens of times, and it doesn't beep. And we're going past hundreds of movies. Really good movies. Movies I like really really love. And I start getting nervous. There's only a couple shelves to go. And I run the scanner over *Andrei Rublev* and nothing happens. And then I run it over *Fanny and Alexander* and I can't believe it, but...nothing happens.

And then I think to myself: I'm going to hell.

I haven't truly like, loved or whatever in the right way, I thought I did, but I didn't, and I'm going to hell. And then I'm on the last shelf of movies and I've already like completely lost lost hope at this point but then suddenly the scanner starts beeping and beeping and I look at the movie that made it beep and it's this like old cruddy VHS tape of *Honeymoon in Vegas*.

(pause)

Honeymoon in Vegas?

(pause)

It's like this terrible movie with Nicholas Cage and Sarah Jessica Parker from like 1989. I was obsessed with it when I was like four. I watched it at my cousin's birthday party.

It's like a really really bad movie.

(pause)

And at first I'm like: what? My entire life can be represented by *Honeymoon in Vegas*? *Honeymoon in Vegas* is like the one movie I truly truly loved? But then I'm like, wait, it doesn't matter, I'm going to heaven. I must have done something right in my life because I'm going to heaven.

And that feeling of like...of like knowing that I made the right choices, was like the best feeling I've ever had.

(a long pause)

Yeah.

(pause)

Yeah.

(A long pause.)

AVERY. ...Okay.

I guess like...

Well, yesterday I had this thought.

I was like: okay.

Maybe it's never gonna get better.

Maybe I'm gonna live with my dad for the rest of my life and like the *actual* problem is just that I'm waiting for things to change.

Like maybe I'm just gonna be that weird depressed guy and I should just like accept it.

And that'll be the life I get.

And that'll be okay.

(a long pause)

Yeah.

(he laughs and rubs a few tears out of his eyes)

Yeah.

(pause)

No. That's okay. I think I can wait until Tuesday. I just wanted one more phone—

(pause)

Uh-huh.

Well, I hope you're having a good vacation.

Sorry that you have to talk to me during it.

(he winces, pause)

No, I didn't…sorry. Yeah. I know that.

I was just—

It was like a stupid joke.

(pause)

Yeah.

I know that.

Yeah.

(He listens intently. Blackout.)

Scene Seven

(A day later. **SAM** *and* **AVERY** *are standing, holding their brooms, in the middle of the aisle. They are gazing up at the tile ceiling, which now has an ominous gap in it.)*

SAM. ...It happened on Sunday.

(They stare at it for a while.)

SAM. Brian and Rebecca are working, it's the matinee, ho hum, ho hum, there's just a few people in the audience, and out of nowhere this huge chunk of tile...

(he points to the gap in the ceiling)

...comes crashing down and LANDS ON THE SEAT NEXT TO SOME OLD LADY.

Like two more inches to the right and she'd be dead.

Apparently there was plaster all over her old lady sweater.

AVERY. Did she—she could sue, right?

Can you sue over that kind of thing?

SAM. Probably. Probably. But Brian is like this huge charmer, apparently Brian just like *turned on the charm* and calmed her down and gave her a voucher for like six free popcorns and six free sodas which by the way he just like drew himself on a receipt or something so if an old lady comes in with a weird cartoon that says she gets a free popcorn or soda give it to her no questions asked.

AVERY. He didn't even give her free tickets?

SAM. He didn't even do that.

(They gaze up at the ceiling for a long time.)

SAM. It's a liability.

It's a huge liability.

It's—someone's gonna get killed and then what.

AVERY. Can't he just put in a new ceiling?

SAM. Well.

>   These are the questions a normal person would ask.

>   But we're talking about Steve.

>   Steve will never spend a dime on anything.

>   Steve would rather this place burn down than he like spend a little money to make it safe or have a nacho machine at concessions.

>   Wouldn't that be nice?

>   If we could make those nachos with the little cheese squirter thing?

>   I keep telling him to get one of those.

>   *(They go back to sweeping.)*

SAM. We haven't sold out a single show since *Slumdog Millionaire.*

>   It's pathetic.

>   *(They sweep for a while. Silence.)*

AVERY. Oh.

>   So. Uh.

>   I went up to the booth the other day and I, uh…

>   I didn't realize there were so many old reels up there.

SAM. Oh yeah. Steve's such a sketchball. He's supposed to send them back to the distributor.

>   And they're all like sitting up there collecting dust. Some of them are really old.

AVERY. There's a lot of good stuff up there.

SAM. I guess.

AVERY. I uh…

>   This is probably a stupid idea.

>   But.

>   Uh.

I was thinking that on uh…

I was thinking on Friday it might be fun to like…we could like just stay here after the last show and watch one or two of em.

(short pause)

Like I saw *Goodfellas* and *Boogie Nights* and a couple other—

(nervously)

It would just be awesome to see them on like the big screen. I've only watched *Goodfellas* on my computer which is pretty like blasphemous when you think about it.

(pause)

It's fine if like you're busy or not interested or whatever.

(**SAM** *is still sweeping.*)

SAM. No. No. That sounds…that sounds cool. I just uh…I'm not gonna be here this weekend.

AVERY. Oh.

SAM. Yeah. Rose will be here if you need help with anything…Steve didn't tell you?

AVERY. No.

SAM. Uch. He's an idiot.

(a short pause)

Yeah. It's not that hard with two people. Rose will come early and help you with set-up and box office and stuff and then you'll just do clean-up on your own.

AVERY. Oh. Yeah./Okay—

SAM. You've been here three weeks so I assumed you felt comfortable with everything/and—

AVERY. Oh, yeah. Yeah. Sure.

SAM. Steve should pay you double but of course he won't. So you'll just get my dinner money.

AVERY. You don't need/to—

SAM. No, that's the way it works.

> *(Pause.)*

AVERY. Where are you going?

> *(A short and unnecessarily weird pause.)*

SAM. …My brother is getting married.

AVERY. Oh! Wow.

SAM. Yeah.

> In Connecticut.
>
> Right outside Bridgeport.

AVERY. Congratulations.

SAM. Yeah.

AVERY. And your whole family is going?

SAM. Yeah. Yeah.

AVERY. Cool.

> *(pause)*
>
> Older or younger?

SAM. What?

AVERY. Older or younger?

SAM. Oh. Um. Older.

> Yeah.
>
> He's 39.
>
> *(Pause.)*

AVERY. Do you like the woman?

SAM. What?

AVERY. Do you like the woman he's marrying?

SAM. Uh. Yeah. I mean, I don't know. I've never met her.

AVERY. Oh.

> *(A long silence, during which they go back to cleaning.)*

AVERY. What's your brother's name?

SAM. Jesse.

> *(Another long pause while they keep cleaning.)*

SAM. *(casually)* He's retarded.

(*A short, confused pause.*)

AVERY. Do you mean/like he's—

SAM. Like in the actual definition of the word.

AVERY. Oh! Okay.

SAM. She's retarded too.

The woman he's marrying.

AVERY. …Okay.

SAM. They met at this uh residential uh facility in Connecticut.

AVERY. Cool. Cool.

SAM. Yeah.

AVERY. Um. They must like each other a lot.

SAM. I guess.

(*Pause.*)

AVERY. Is it…does he have Down's /Syndrome?

SAM. No.

He's just uh—

He's basically like the—he's basically like a third grader.

AVERY. Oh.

(*Pause. More sweeping.*)

SAM. *(a confession)* I don't know him all that well.

(**ROSE** *enters with a yo-yo.*)

AVERY. *(trying to politely end the conversation)* Well!

Next weekend maybe.

ROSE. Next weekend maybe what?

AVERY. Uh.

We were thinking of staying past closing on Friday and watching *Goodfellas*.

ROSE. Oh yeah. We have that upstairs.

AVERY. But Sam's gonna be away so I was saying maybe /
next—

ROSE. *I'll* stay and watch it with you.

(**SAM**, *who has been standing in the second row, sits
down heavily in one of the seats and closes his eyes.*)

AVERY. *(glancing over at* **SAM***)* Oh...Uh—

AVERY. I don't know...maybe we should wait for Sam and
then we can /all—

ROSE. Well we don't have to watch *Goodfellas*. We could
watch something else. There's *Mulholland Drive*. That
movie is hot. And some older ones too from before it
was The Flick.

I'm totally free on Friday. Let's do it.

(**SAM***'s face is no longer visible to* **ROSE** *and* **AVERY***; he
faces the movie screen and stares up at it, beseechingly.*)

AVERY. Uh. Yeah. Sure. Okay.

ROSE. Awesome.

Yes.

We should like bring music and have like a rockin'
dance party.

(**SAM** *closes his eyes.*)

ROSE. Hey. Look what I like unearthed from my closet.

(*She holds up the yo-yo.*)

ROSE. I'm totally gonna bring the yo-yo back in style.

(*She yo-yos for a while, a simple up and down.*)

ROSE. I only know how to do this, though.

AVERY. Here. Let me try.

(**ROSE** *gives* **AVERY** *the yo-yo and he does something
sort of impressive...maybe he walks the dog? Or flips it
around and catches it.*)

ROSE. YES!! OH MY GOD!! I love it.

(**AVERY** *hands it back to her, blushing.*)

ROSE. Where are you gonna be this weekend, Sam?

SAM. *(flatly, still facing forward)* ...My brother's wedding.

ROSE. Where?

SAM. Bridgeport.

ROSE. Cool.

> *(**ROSE** glances at the back of **SAM**'s head, clocking that he's being a little weird, and then exits. **AVERY** gathers up his broom and dustpan and heads towards the door.)*

AVERY. Hey. Uh. I keep meaning to ask. Did you ever find out what was going on with your skin?

> *(**SAM** is still sitting and facing forward during the next speech.)*

SAM. Yeah.

> I went to the doctor.
>
> *(a short pause)*
>
> It's called Pityriasis Rosea.
>
> *(a short pause)*
>
> It's not contagious.
>
> *(a short pause)*
>
> It looks like a fungus but it's not.
>
> *(a short pause)*
>
> They don't know what causes it but you get it all over your torso and it itches like fuck and it lasts 6-8 weeks.

AVERY. Ah man.

SAM. The good news is you only get it once in your life.

> *(He stands up and lifts up the back of shirt so **AVERY** can see it.)*

AVERY. Whoa!

SAM. The spots make like a—if the spots are in a distinctive christmas tree formation you know it's Pityriasis Rosea.

AVERY. Wow. Wow. That looks pretty bad.

> *(**SAM** lowers his shirt.)*

SAM. *(depressed)* Yeah. It's not though.

AVERY. You want box office or refreshments?

(A long pause while **SAM** *contemplates this)*

SAM. Box office.

(After a few seconds, **SAM** *slowly gets up and they start to exit together.* **ROSE** *enters the projection booth and we see her moving around in the window.)*

*(***SAM** *stands in the aisle and looks up at her.)*

*(***AVERY** *waits by the door.)*

*(***SAM** *tears his gaze away from the projection booth, and they leave together.)*

(The door slams shut.)

(Blackout.)

Scene Eight

(Friday night. Darkness. The last movie is ending. The very end of the credits. A flash of green. A flash of white. Then the lights come on automatically. We see **ROSE** *in the projection booth.)*

(After a few seconds **AVERY** *comes in the door, dragging the yellow mop bucket and mop.)*

(He starts cleaning.)

(He starts on his side of the aisle and mops. He encounters a large popcorn bag and throws it away. He mops more.)

(He glances up at the projection booth. **ROSE** *is moving around, doing something. She sees him and pumps her fist in the air in a "we're gonna party" gesture.* **AVERY** *tries to smile.)*

(He moves to the left side of the theater and starts cleaning.)

*(***ROSE** *knocks on the window and holds up a CD, wiggling her eyebrows.* **AVERY** *shrugs and shakes his head, like, "what are you saying?")*

(Inside the projection booth (we probably can't see this), **ROSE** *inserts the CD into the sound system.)*

(An extremely danceable hip-hop classic from the past decade comes blasting into the theater. Maybe Jay-Z's "I Just Wanna Love U." ***AVERY** *is startled. He tries to keep sweeping. He's not sure what is happening.)*

*(***ROSE** *leaves the projection booth, and 10 seconds later kicks through the door, grooving to the music.)*

ROSE. Dance party!!

---

*Please see Music Use Note on page 3

(**AVERY** *laughs anxiously.*)

(**ROSE** *grooves down the aisle.* **AVERY** *bobs his head up and down, trying to look supportive.*)

ROSE. Come on!!

(**AVERY** *shakes his head no, still bobbing supportively.*)

(**ROSE** *rolls her eyes, disappointed, but then proceeds to do a totally awesome improvised dance in the aisle and maybe even in some of the rows. She's really wild and weird and uninhibited. It's pretty cathartic. It should be different every night. Maybe she incorporates a couple moves from bhangra and/or hip hop and/or West African dance classes in her past. This lasts about two minutes.* **AVERY** *stands in his row, bobbing his head the whole time.*)

(*Finally* **ROSE** *tuckers herself out. The song is still blasting.*)

ROSE. WHEW!

(*She runs out of the room, through the door, and up to the projection booth, where she turns the music off. Then she comes back down and reenters.*)

ROSE. …Aaaanyway.

AVERY. That was great.

ROSE. Yeah.

Whatever.

I feel like an idiot now.

AVERY. No, no.

Sorry I didn't like—

Sorry I didn't like join in.

(*A weird pause.*)

ROSE. So what do you wanna do?

AVERY. Oh.

Ah.

We could watch a movie?
Or—

ROSE. You wanna get stoned?

AVERY. Ah…no. Thank you.

ROSE. You sure?

AVERY. Yes.

I get really…I get really freaked out. I get really angry.

ROSE. Awesome.

AVERY. No. Not awesome. I like sit in a corner and refuse to talk to anyone.

(a short pause)

The last time I smoked pot it was the end of freshman year at this like huge party and I like found this guy's collection of Calvin and Hobbes and sat in his closet and read them all night and if people tried to talk to me I was like: LEAVE ME THE FUCK ALONE!!

ROSE. You go to Clark, right?

AVERY. Yeah. Well. I took this past semester off. But yeah.

ROSE. Expensive.

AVERY. I actually have a free ride.

ROSE. Really?

AVERY. My dad teaches there. He's head of his department, so—

ROSE. What does he teach?

AVERY. Uh. Linguistics…Semiotics…

ROSE. I have no idea what that is.

AVERY. *(trying to laugh)* Yeah.

ROSE. I went to Fitchburg State.

AVERY. Cool.

Cool.

ROSE. You still live at home?

AVERY. Oh. Well. Yeah. For now, while I'm taking time off from Clark, but when I go back /I'll—

ROSE. I'm not judging. I lived at home until I was twenty-one.

(*pause*)

Sam still lives at home.

AVERY. He does?

ROSE. Yeah.

AVERY. Huh.

ROSE. When he first started working here he had this like super-controlling girlfriend and I think he lived with her in like Athol or something? She would like show up and like give me these insane paranoid looks. You know, like one of those women who's always like: "are you gonna steal my boyfriend?!"

And then they broke up—I think he broke up with her?—and he moved back in with his parents. He lives in the attic or something.

AVERY. Huh.

I guess he like...he doesn't tell me a lot. He seems pretty private.

ROSE. Yeah. He's weird.

AVERY. I mean, I like him a lot.

ROSE. Yeah. I mean, me too.

(*Pause.*)

AVERY. Did you know that his brother is retarded?

ROSE. WHAT?!!

AVERY. Yeah. Oh. Maybe I shouldn't have told you that.

ROSE. REALLY?!

AVERY. I mean it's not a big deal.

ROSE. I did *not* know that.

(*Pause.*)

ROSE. Like how is he retarded?

AVERY. I don't know.

I mean, I think he's just um…

(a pause)

I think he's just retarded.

(Pause.)

ROSE. My ex-boyfriend had a cousin with Down's Syndrome and she always liked to flash people her tits.

Like I went to their family reunion this one summer and she like flashed me her tits like seventeen times.

And I would be like: "Awesome, Ruth, thank you" and I would try not to like stare at her like weird nipples.

*(A long pause, in which **AVERY** does a number of mental calculations.)*

AVERY. Your ex-boyfriend?

ROSE. Yeah.

AVERY. Huh.

AVERY. For some reason I uh…

(Pause.)

AVERY. I think someone told me that you were, uh…

I think someone told me that you were gay.

ROSE. Oh.

No.

I mean, whatever, I've been with girls a couple times.

But no.

(Long weird pause.)

ROSE. You wanna watch a movie?

AVERY. *(relieved)* Yeah! Yes. Definitely.

(She stands up.)

Hey. Uh. Would you ever show me how to use the projector?

ROSE. It's just like a shitty old 35 mill.

AVERY. No, no...I'm like...that's why I wanted to work here. This is one of the only theaters left in Worcester County that has—yeah. I'm obsessed with film, and like old...

I actually refused to work at any of the theaters that just do digital.

ROSE. But everything's gonna be digital. In like six months. Seriously. Steve is an idiot. If he doesn't go digital or sell this place in the next year it'll shut down.

AVERY. Yeah, I like...I guess I disagree. Or like, I think that's really immoral.

ROSE. What is?

AVERY. Projecting a movie made on film through a digital projector.

ROSE. I dunno.

(short pause)

I mean, I guess I personally like...like apart from this job I never go to the movies.

(short pause)

I'm kind of over movies.

(short pause)

I used to be super-into them but now I'm over them.

(This is all really depressing AVERY.)

ROSE. You're totally obsessed with them, aren't you?

AVERY. Yeah.

I mean.

They're like my life.

ROSE. Huh.

(A short pause.)

ROSE. Well, I'll show you how to do it. You can fill in for me when I'm sick or whatever and then eventually Steve'll promote you.

AVERY. Seriously?

ROSE. Yeah. Sure. Sam keeps bugging me to show him how to do it but I bet you'd be better 'cuz you're so obsessed with it.

(ROSE *starts walking up the aisle.* AVERY *stays back, guiltily, thinking of* SAM.)

(*She turns around.*)

ROSE. Come on!

(*He follows. They leave the theater, disappear for about 15 seconds, and then reappear in the window of the projection booth. They move around, then disappear (looking in the storage closet?), then reappear with a giant reel of film.*)

(*Through the window, we watch* ROSE *teach* AVERY *how to thread the projector. He probably does it himself while she watches and provides instructions. He is smiling. They finish threading the projector. They turn it on. A movie begins; we see the green light, then blackness, then the opening credit sequence, music. It is the 6 minute-long opening credit sequence music from "The Wild Bunch."*)

(AVERY *watches the beginning of the movie, his face almost pressed up against the projection booth window, and then he and* ROSE *exit and come through the theater door again.*)

(AVERY *doesn't take his eyes off the screen while he walks down the aisle. He finds the third row, stage left, and sits in the center.*)

(ROSE *follows him and sits next to him.*)

(*They watch the movie for about 45 seconds.*)

(*Then* ROSE *very slowly turns her face and looks at* AVERY. *He notices this but continues watching the screen, attempting to appear nonchalant.*)

(ROSE *keeps looking at* AVERY. AVERY *keeps looking at the screen.*)

(*After a while,* ROSE *leans over and kisses* AVERY*'s neck.*)

(AVERY *is frozen, still watching the movie. He does not move away.*)

(ROSE *keeps kissing* AVERY*'s neck, contemplates nibbling his ear, decides against it, and goes back to looking at him.*)

(AVERY *keeps watching the movie.*)

(ROSE *takes her index finger and traces little stripes and circles on* AVERY*'s neck. Then she takes her finger and runs it in a straight line down* AVERY*'s shirt (or maybe she stops to make tiny circles around his nipples?). Then her hand disappears from our view.*)

(AVERY *is still watching the screen.*)

(ROSE *unzips his pants and begins to touch him.* AVERY *lets her touch him and does not take his eyes off the screen.*)

(*This goes on for a minute or so but something is clearly off and eventually* ROSE *slowly takes her hand away, and, mortified, goes back to watching the movie.*)

(AVERY *keeps watching the movie. He might start crying. He doesn't.*)

(*Eventually* ROSE *gets up, walks up the aisle (*AVERY *does not turn around), and ten seconds later we see her in the projection booth. She shuts off the movie and the lights in the theater automatically go on.*)

(*As if released from a spell,* AVERY *bends over, elbows on knees, and covers his face in shame.*)

(He stays this way while **ROSE** *comes back downstairs, walks down the aisle, and sits in the row across from him, in the aisle seat.)*

(A long silence.)

ROSE. Sorry.

AVERY. No.

I'm sorry.

(Short pause.)

AVERY. Oh my god.

I wanna kill myself.

ROSE. Wow.

Thanks.

*(***AVERY*** *removes his face from his hands and looks at* **ROSE**. *Another long silence.)*

ROSE. I um…

Yeah.

Wow.

We can just forget that this ever happened, okay?

(Pause.)

ROSE. I feel like I like *molested* you or something.

AVERY. You didn't molest me.

ROSE. Yeah.

I'm an idiot.

(a short pause)

Honestly, I don't know why I even like *did* that.

I wasn't planning on doing that.

I swear to god.

(a short pause)

There's something wrong with me.

AVERY. No, there's something wrong with *me*.

(A long silence.)

ROSE. Well are we just gonna like sit here and like freak out together in silence?

Because then I'd /rather—

AVERY. It's just.

This has happened to me.

Before.

(Pause.)

AVERY. So don't feel—please don't feel/like—

ROSE. Yeah, but you weren't giving me the vibe and I went for it anyway.

(A long pause.)

ROSE. …So you/like—

AVERY. I just have a hard time.

Sometimes.

When like—my mind goes blank and I like…

I always just think: I'd rather be watching a movie.

(His elbows go onto his knees and his face goes into his hands again.)

ROSE. It's okay, Avery.

(She moves across the aisle and sits next to him again.)

ROSE. What do you think about when you, like, fantasize?

(No response. After a pause:)

ROSE. Do you ever think about/guys?

AVERY. I really don't want to answer these questions.

ROSE. Okay.

That's okay.

(His face is still in his hands. ROSE leans back in her seat, almost relaxed now, and props her feet up on the seat in front of her.)

ROSE. Well, I'm fucked up too.

AVERY. *(muffled)* Yeah?

(*Short pause.*)

ROSE. I can't stay attracted to anyone for longer than four months.

AVERY. ...Huh.

ROSE. At first I'm like this like crazy nymphomaniac. All I want do is like have sex all the time.

Like eight, nine times a day.

AVERY. Whoa.

ROSE. And then it like totally goes away and I turn into like this like dead fish.

And then I like fake it until we break up.

AVERY. Huh.

(*A long pause.*)

ROSE. And you know what's even weirder?

AVERY. What?

ROSE. When I like fantasize I just like think about *myself.*

(*A long pause.*)

AVERY. Really?

ROSE. Yeah. Like everyone else is blurry except for me.

I'm like totally in focus.

And I like look amazing.

And everyone is like: holy shit.

That girl looks so amazing.

(*Pause.*)

ROSE. It's really embarrassing.

AVERY. I don't think it's embarrassing at all.

(*Silence. They both are leaning back in their seats now, facing the blank screen, peaceful, arms touching.*)

AVERY. Can we just sit here for a little while?

ROSE. Yeah.

Yeah.

Of course.

(A long, much more comfortable silence.)

AVERY. Today is the one-year anniversary of the day I tried to kill myself.

(After a pause:)

ROSE. Really?

AVERY. Uh-huh.

(Pause.)

ROSE. How did you do it?

AVERY. I swallowed a bunch of pins.

ROSE. Oh my god.

(Pause.)

That *works?*

AVERY. Well.

(short pause)

I didn't plan on doing it.

(short pause)

It was a weird day.

(A long pause.)

ROSE. Huh. I've been like super super sad before but I've never wanted to commit suicide.

I just like don't get it.

I don't get suicide.

It's like: aren't you curious what's gonna like *happen* to you? In like the future? I'm just like so curious about my future.

AVERY. Yeah.

You've probably never…

(He decides not to say it.)

AVERY. ...You know what *I* don't get?

ROSE. What?

AVERY. Bulimia.

ROSE. Oh my god!! I know, right?!

AVERY. Barfing is so horrible.

ROSE. I know!! It's like /the—

AVERY. It's like the worst feeling in the world. It's like being in hell.

ROSE. I know! Like why would you like *voluntarily*...like if you're gonna like have an eating disorder just be anorexic.

(Pause.)

ROSE. This is an awesome conversation.

(Pause.)

AVERY. I almost quit my second day working here.

ROSE. Why?

AVERY. I just like...I couldn't get out of bed. The first day was just like really awkward and I couldn't remember anything and I like...I had no idea how to hold the broom—

*(**ROSE** laughs.)*

AVERY. I'm serious. And then I woke up the next day and just like freaked out. I was like: I can't have a job. I'm way too depressed. And I didn't get out of bed and I like lay there under the covers staring up at the ceiling and 4 pm rolled around, I like watched the numbers on my alarm clock, and I was like, I should be at The Flick by now, but I couldn't even bring myself to call in sick. And then it was like 4:05, and then it was 4:10, and I was like that's it, I just lost my first job, I give up. And then—it's weird—I didn't even make the decision—but it was like—the second I thought, like—I give up—my body started moving and I like pushed the blanket off and like stood up and put on my uniform and like walked outside and walked to the bus and took the bus and walked in here and made up some like lie to Sam about why I was late and that was it.

(A long pause.)

ROSE. So why are you depressed?

AVERY. Are you serious?

ROSE. Yeah.

AVERY. Um. Because everything is horrible? And sad?

(a short pause)

And the answer to every terrible situation always seems to be like, Be Yourself, but I have no idea what that fucking means. Who's Myself? Apparently there's some like amazing awesome person deep down inside of me or something? I have no idea who that guy is. I'm always faking it. And it looks to me like everyone else is faking it too. Like everyone is acting out some stereotype of like…exactly…who you'd think they be'd be. Everyone's acting like they're on a sitcom or something. All the time. And I had one friend, one friend, at Clark, this guy from Bangladesh who was really into sculpture, and then he transferred to RISD at the end of freshman year.

(After a short pause:)

AVERY. And my mom like…

AVERY. Actually never mind.

(A pause.)

ROSE. Do you think *I'm* a stereotype?

AVERY. Of like—

ROSE. Of like—whatever.

Of like what I am.

AVERY. …Yeah.

ROSE. You do?!

AVERY. Yeah.

(Pause.)

ROSE. I guess you're right.

   (Pause.)

ROSE. Uch.

   (Pause.)

ROSE. Wait.

   Were you being fake? Just now?

AVERY. When?

ROSE. When you were like…when you were going off about how everyone is so fake. Were you faking it then?

AVERY. I mean yes and no.

   It's hard to tell, I guess.

ROSE. Yeah.

   *(They look up at the blank screen and prop their knees up on the seats in front of them. Maybe **ROSE** puts her head on **AVERY**'s shoulder.)*

   (Blackout.)

   (Jeanne Moreau singing "Le Tourbillon" plays.)

End of Act One.

ACT TWO

Scene One

(Three days later. SAM and AVERY, each on their side of the aisle, sweeping. SAM is in the middle of a seemingly big dramatic story.)

SAM. — so the next day we all went to see a movie. I mean minus my brother and his girlfriend. Wife. We went to this huge like multiplex outside of Bridgeport.

AVERY. What movie?

SAM. The new Daniel Craig thing—/ *State of*—

AVERY. Was it good?

SAM. It was okay.

It was okay.

Anyway. On the way there I stopped at this Mexican takeout place that I read about online. It's like this famous Bridgeport tamale place. And then...

I brought the tamales into the theater.

AVERY. You hate when /people—

SAM. I know. I know. This is the point of—I know. But we were in a huge hurry and I didn't want to eat them in my aunt's car 'cause she has this like pristine like fucking Passat that she's all obsessive about and I wanted to like you know you know pour the little cups of red and green salsa all over the tamales etcetera etcetera. So I decide to bring the bag of tamales with me into the movie theater. But then we can't find parking and we're you know late and there's a weirdly long line for tickets. And we don't actually sit down in the theater until halfway through the previews. So

71

after we sit down I open my like Styrofoam container and get in a few delicious bites of tamale before the movie starts. But then I put it away. Because I'm like you know like philosophically opposed to rustling your plastic bags and like squeaking your Styrofoam container during the actual movie. So I put the tamales back in the plastic bag and I put the plastic bag on the floor. And we're like five minutes into the movie when this woman comes like uh like waddling down the aisle into the theater. And this is gonna sound horrible but she's uh…she's like really really smelly. Like one of the smelliest people I've ever…uh, smelled. Like she's not homeless or anything, it's not like the homeless pee smell, it's more like a…a kind of like…it's kind of like a chunky cheesy kind of smell?

AVERY. Oh god. Okay. I get it.

SAM. And she sits right in front of us.

And I am…I am like *incredibly sensitive* to people's smells.

When I was a kid my dad had this friend who had halitosis and I couldn't even like be in the same room as him.

AVERY. Wait. Do you—

Have I ever smelled bad to you?

SAM. You have never smelled bad to me.

AVERY. You promise?

SAM. I promise.

I mean a couple of times I smelled your very pleasant smelling shampoo but that's it.

AVERY. Okay.

SAM. Anyway, this lady sits down right in front of us and her cheesy smell keeps coming at me in like waves and I can't focus on the movie and I start going crazy. And my mom and I are whispering about it and then we convince my dad and my aunt and my cousins that we should move seats. And so we all get up like a bunch of assholes and move five rows back.

AVERY. Did you bring the tamales with you?

SAM. That's the—no. I didn't. The point is that I was so freaked out by not being able to pay attention to Daniel Craig and getting away from the smelly woman that I totally forgot all about the tamales. And then we watch the movie and then it ends and the credits are rolling. And we're all collecting our things and getting ready to go when I notice these middle-aged ladies five rows in front of me, not the smelly lady, the ladies who were sitting to the left of us originally, and they're all getting ready to go.

And they start walking towards the aisle and then one of them goes: "Linda, are these yours?" And the other one goes, "No. Trish, are they yours?" And Trish or whoever is like "No I didn't bring anything in" and I look and I see they're holding up my bag of tamales.

And then I realize: I'm that douchebag.

I'm that douchebag who brings like random weird ethnic food into a movie theater and then forgets about it and leaves it there!

I am my own worst nightmare!

And I sit there paralyzed, watching them ask each other, is this yours? is this yours? And I'm too scared to say anything and then eventually Linda or whoever just takes the bag and they all walk up the aisle together and when they get to the doors *she throws it in the trash.*

She throws it away for me.

(Pause.)

AVERY. Okay…

(Pause.)

SAM. That's the story.

AVERY. I don't get it.

SAM. It's like…it's like I was dead or something. I was watching the world like go on without me.

AVERY. But if you were dead you wouldn't have left the bag of tamales /on the—

SAM. No. But I was like…

(A long pause.)

SAM. It all made more sense in my head.

(Pause.)

SAM. It was like a really good story in my head.

(Pause.)

SAM. It felt like some profound like realization and now I can't remember what the realization was.

*(**ROSE** enters.)*

ROSE. How was the wedding?

SAM. Oh.

It was okay.

ROSE. What'd you wear?

SAM. Uh…a suit.

(Pause.)

ROSE. Soooo…

I think Steve's trying to sell it.

(They look at her.)

ROSE. The Flick.

I think he's trying to sell it.

AVERY. …No.

ROSE. I came in early yesterday and he was here with some like businessy guy talking about how the lobby had "promise." Then after the guy left I was like what the fuck is going on and Steve was like "I might be moving to Tucson."

SAM. Whoa.

ROSE. I bet he's selling it cause he can't get any distributors to send him stuff anymore.

AVERY. Who would he sell it to?

ROSE. I don't know. Probably Fuckface 500.

AVERY. You mean Loews? AMC?

ROSE. I have no idea.

SAM. Huh.

AVERY. He can't sell it.

That would be like one of the saddest things of all time.

SAM. Uh…

I think the *Holocaust* is one of the saddest things of all time.

AVERY. The big guys wouldn't buy it. It's just one screen. It wouldn't make financial sense.

It must be a smaller chain.

It was just one guy with him in the lobby?

ROSE. Yeah.

AVERY. Did he say anything about going digital?

ROSE. Nope.

I didn't ask.

AVERY. If he goes digital your job will be obsolete.

ROSE. I'll be happy if he sells it.

AVERY. Why?

ROSE. Because this place is a piece of shit. And Steve is a retard.

(Then she catches herself and blushes.)

ROSE. *(to SAM)* Sorry.

(Pause.)

ROSE. I'm gonna go upstairs.

(to SAM) I'm glad you had a nice time with your family.

(She leaves. **SAM** *clocks all of this, frowns, then dumps something in the trash.)*

AVERY. That's unbelievable. If they go digital I might have to like…I might have to quit.

(Pause. They go back to cleaning, then:)

SAM. Did you tell Rose about my brother?

(Pause.)

AVERY. You /mean—

SAM. You know what I mean.

(Pause.)

AVERY. Uh—

SAM. Yeah. It's cool. It's cool. I just like mentioned that to you in confidence, you know?

(Pause.)

AVERY. Sorry.

I didn't know.

SAM. You didn't know *what?*

(Pause.)

SAM. Did you tell her like—what did you tell her?

AVERY. I just said that he was um…

(pause)

I'm really sorry.

(Pause.)

SAM. Yeah. Whatever.

Who cares.

I just had like a fucking shitty weekend.

I hate weddings, anyway, so.

(Pause.)

SAM. My mother went like way over the top. It was disgusting.

It was like—you're the one who fucking sent him away and then there were like—there were like cookies in little cloth bags with like my brother and his wife's like fucking initials stenciled on them.

And it's like, great, Mom. Now you have even more fucking credit card debt.

(Pause. He tries to go back to cleaning, but then:)

SAM. And it was like—everyone was acting so happy.

Like trying so hard.

Like oh this whole fucking charade is so fucking joyful.

(pause)

And it's like the only *actually* happy people here are retarded!

The rest of you are just miserable fucks.

(Long pause. They sweep.)

SAM. And everyone always pretends like the catering is so good!

Like oh my god the food is so *good*, isn't it?

And I'm like: it was shitty!

It was shitty lukewarm food cooked for 115 people!

Can't we just admit that wedding food is always a little shitty?

(Pause.)

SAM. If I ever have a wedding I'm gonna like have food trucks come and like set up outside the wedding tent and people can line up one by one and order tacos.

AVERY. That sounds good.

SAM. Maybe like one taco truck and then one shawarma truck.

AVERY. I would do massive amounts of take-out Chinese.

SAM. Huh.

(Pause.)

SAM. Did you have a good time with Rose?

AVERY. Yeah. Sure.

SAM. What'd you watch?

AVERY. Oh. Uh.

>*The Wild Bunch.*

>Yeah.

>She'd never seen it before.

>Jesus.

>If Steve sells this place to some like chain that'll be so depressing.

SAM. Did you guys like hang out afterwards?

AVERY. Uh. A little.

SAM. Why are you being weird?

>Did you guys like give each other like *handjobs* or something?

AVERY. *(laughing)* No! God, no.

>Jesus.

>Sam.

>We just talked.

SAM. What'd you talk about?

AVERY. Nothing.

>*(A pause. More sweeping.)*

AVERY. Oh.

>I thought you might be—

>It turns out she's straight? Or bi. I'm not sure.

SAM. Excuse me?

AVERY. I mean, not that it matters.

>But she told me that she's not a lesbian.

>Didn't you say she—

>**(ROSE** *enters.)*

ROSE. Avery. I forgot.

Can you cover for me for the first hour on Thursday?

I know, I'm already taking advantage of you.

AVERY. *(quick paranoid glance at* SAM*)* Uh. Sure. Yeah. Of course.

ROSE. Cool.

Oh, and I watched that *Four Nights of a Dreamer* movie.

You're right.

It was *amazing.*

(She leaves.)

(A long silence. SAM *stares after her, then turns to* AVERY *and stares at him.)*

*(*AVERY *tries to say something but is too terrified.)*

SAM. Did she show you how to use the projector?

(Pause.)

AVERY. Well. I was really curious. I mean. I was actually just interested in how it *worked,* not um in um getting promoted or anything but then she said she could train me to be the uh the uh alternate and I didn't feel like I could—

*(*SAM *picks up a half-eaten bag of popcorn off his side of the theater, walks slowly across the aisle to* AVERY*'s side of the theater, rips the bag open and and then flings it gloriously into* AVERY*'s area, popcorn showering everywhere.)*

(Then he stalks out of the theater and slams the door behind him.)

*(*AVERY *stands there for a while.)*

*(*ROSE *moves around in the projection booth, threading the next film into the projector.)*

(Blackout.)

Scene Two

(The end of the night.)

*(***SAM*** *and* ***AVERY*** *are in the middle of mopping.)*

*(***SAM*** *is giving* ***AVERY*** *the silent treatment.)*

(They mop in terrible silence together.)

(Occasionally they each have to go squeeze out their mop in the yellow bucket and listen to the horrible squeezing dripping sound.)

(Then the sound of the mop slopping down against the floor.)

(This goes on for a while.)

*(***ROSE*** *is in the projection booth, moving around, unwinding the film.)*

(She comes downstairs.)

(She sits on the edge of a seat in the last row, ***AVERY****'s row.)*

(She takes some money out and counts it underneath her breath.)

ROSE. 10, 20, 30, 33 ...

God.

(pause)

11 each.

(She hands money to ***AVERY****. She walks over to* ***SAM*** *and tries to hand him money, but he is furiously mopping. She puts the money down on the armrest of the seat nearest to him.)*

ROSE. Could one of you give me a ride home tonight?

My sister borrowed my car.

*(***SAM*** *continues mopping. After a pause:)*

AVERY. Oh. Um. My dad is picking me up.

ROSE. Sam?

(He doesn't respond. He continues mopping.)

ROSE. Sam.

(No response.)

AVERY. But.

Um.

I guess I could ask him if he'd take you back to Boylston.

ROSE. Sam.

What the fuck.

(SAM mops some more. Then he walks over to the mop bucket. He squeezes the mop in the mop bucket with tremendous power. Then he dips it in the water and squeezes it again. ROSE and AVERY watch him do this. SAM does not take his eyes off the mop when he finally says:)

SAM. *(quietly)* Why'd you show Avery how to do the projector?

(Pause.)

SAM. What the fuck is *wrong* with you?

AVERY. Uh.

I'm gonna go to the bathroom.

(AVERY walks up the aisle and then leaves. ROSE is looking at SAM. SAM is staring into the dirty mop water.)

ROSE. I didn't know you/wanted—

SAM. Yes. Yes you did.

I've been working here for almost twice as long as you and you know Steve only promoted you first because he thinks you're hot.

And three months ago I asked you if you would train/ me and you said—

ROSE. Okay. Okay.

You're right.

I'm sorry.

SAM. Do you know how humiliating it is to be working with like *twenty*-somethings who are rising in the ranks of your shitty job faster than you are?

(Pause.)

ROSE. I'm sorry.

It's—

I was stupid. I wasn't thinking.

I just—

I can train you too. Then if I get sick you can /take turns—

SAM. No. No way.

I'm not interested anymore.

(Pause.)

SAM. No fucking way.

ROSE. O*kay*.

(Pause. SAM is starting to look ill.)

ROSE. So. What.

Are you gonna like hate my guts now?

(After a pause:)

SAM. *(quietly)* Oh god.

ROSE. What's going on?

SAM. I feel sick.

I feel like I'm gonna…

Oh my god.

*(He sits down in one of the front rows and faces the movie screen, away from **ROSE**.)*

ROSE. Sam.

(Silence.)

SAM. I just…I can't stand it. I can't do it anymore.

(Pause.)

SAM. It's making me nauseous. It's making me sick.

(a short pause)

I'm like breaking out in fucking rashes.

ROSE. I have no idea what you're talking about.

SAM. You don't?

(Pause.)

SAM. Really?

(A long silence.)

SAM. I like—I fucking love you.

*(Pause. **SAM** is still looking out at the movie screen.)*

SAM. I don't even know why.

You're like…

I see all these things that are wrong with you.

But it's like—

(Pause.)

SAM. It's really bad.

It's really bad.

It's not like a—

It goes way beyond the word "crush," or like—

I want to like—

I can't sleep.

I mean, I haven't really slept for like the past year and a half.

And then when I do sleep I dream about you. And you're like talking to me. Or like fucking some other guy. Or standing in front of me in like a motel room like brushing your teeth.

(a short pause)

It's never been like this before.

I walk down the street and all I'm thinking is:

Rose.

Rose.

Rose.

It's like the fucking soundtrack to my life.

Just your name makes me like…

(Silence.)

SAM. I've pictured saying this to you.

I've pictured saying it so many times.

(Pause. He does not turn around. They are both very still.)

ROSE. So what do you want?

(Pause. He is still facing forward.)

SAM. What do you mean?

ROSE. Like what do you think is gonna happen now?

(Pause.)

SAM. I don't know.

(Pause.)

SAM. I guess I just…

I guess I needed to get it off my chest.

ROSE. But is this the kind of thing where you want the person to love you back or you actually secretly *don't* want them to love you back?

(Pause.)

SAM. That's a good question.

ROSE. Because it sort of seems like it has nothing to do with me.

Like *me* me.

You know?

(Pause. SAM's heart breaks.)

SAM. That's not how I wanted it to seem.

Be.

That's not how I wanted it to be.

(ROSE sighs a long, sad sigh.)

ROSE. Like—

Like even right now. It's like you're performing or something.

(Pause.)

SAM. I'm not performing.

(Pause.)

SAM. I'm not performing.

ROSE. So turn around and look at me.

(Pause.)

SAM. *(tears starting to brim in his eyes)* Do you like me back?

ROSE. Oh my god.

(Pause.)

ROSE. Would you please just turn around?

(SAM shakes his head no.)

ROSE. Sam.

(He shakes his head no again.)

ROSE. You're seriously not going to turn around and look at me?

(He does not turn around.)

ROSE. You don't know me.

Like for whatever reason you like me…I'm not like… I'm not like like that at all.

(a short pause)

Trust me.

(a short pause)

Okay?

*(**AVERY** bursts through the door, trying not to dry-heave.*
***ROSE** and **SAM** stand up.)*

AVERY. Oh my god.

(They stare at him.)

AVERY. Someone took a...

Someone took a shit on the floor of the men's
bathroom and they—

(He is bent over.)

AVERY. And they spread it all over the—

It's all over the walls and it—

(He tries to breathe.)

AVERY. I just puked. I just puked on the floor of the
bathroom. I feel like I'm gonna—

*(**SAM** walks up the aisle and takes **AVERY**'s arm.)*

SAM. You gotta sit down.

You gotta sit down and put your head between your
knees.

*(**AVERY** sits down and puts his head between his knees.)*

SAM. You gotta breathe.

Take deep breaths.

AVERY. Oh god.

SAM. I'm gonna take care of it.

(He grabs the mop.)

SAM. You just take it easy.

ROSE. I'll help.

SAM. No. No.

(firmly)

You stay here and you watch him and you get him water. I'm gonna take care of it.

AVERY. You're gonna have to—

Now my puke is all over the place.

(his head swimming)

I'm so sorry.

Are you still mad at me?

SAM. It's fine. I'm not mad at you.

AVERY. It's everywhere.

Why would somebody *do* that?

SAM. This happens.

This kind of thing happens in movie theaters.

I'm gonna deal with it.

AVERY. But you have such a sensitive sense of smell!

SAM. Avery.

Don't worry about it.

I'm totally cool with puke.

I'm totally cool with shit.

I'm gonna take care of it.

(SAM walks up the aisle towards the door. Before exiting he stoically thrusts the mop up into the air like a sword.)

SAM. I'm taking care of it!

(And he exits.)

(AVERY bends over and breathes.)

(ROSE watches him.)

ROSE. You want a cup of water?

AVERY. Yeah.

(he breathes)

That would be great.

(She watches him for a while.)

ROSE. Avery.

Please don't tell Sam about what happened the other night.

AVERY. Of course.

I mean.

You don't either.

ROSE. I won't.

(Pause.)

AVERY. Can I still fill in for you on Thursday night?

(She considers this.)

ROSE. I'll make it work.

(Pause.)

ROSE. Sometimes I worry that there's something really, really wrong with me.

But that I'll never know exactly what it is.

AVERY. Uh.

No. You're fine.

ROSE. Really?

AVERY. Yeah.

(Pause.)

ROSE. I'll get you some water.

(ROSE *walks out of the theater to get water.)*

(Blackout.)

Scene Three

(SAM and AVERY, mid-walkthrough. ROSE is in the projection booth, moving around, threading the projector. Occasionally she stops and tries casually to peer out at them.)

SAM. Have you seen this video everyone is putting up on Facebook?

The one where the water bottle starts talking back to the woman?

AVERY. Uh…no.

I'm not on Facebook.

SAM. Oh.

(Pause.)

SAM. That's funny. I looked for you once and couldn't find you. But then I thought that maybe you were "invisible."

AVERY. I mean, if I was on Facebook we would be Facebook friends. I mean, I would've friended you by now.

SAM. Sure. Sure.

(Pause.)

SAM. What's the objection to Facebook?

Actually. Never mind. I'm tired of hearing the objections to Facebook.

(They go back to sweeping. Then:)

AVERY. I was on it. For a little while. When I was a freshman. But then my mom got on it because I was on it and she started reconnecting with all her friends from high school and then she reconnected with her high school boyfriend and they started writing each other letters and then she left my dad for him.

(Pause.)

SAM. Wait, seriously?

AVERY. Yeah.

> She moved to Atlanta a year and a half ago.

> To be with him.

SAM. To be with her high school sweetheart??!!

AVERY. Yup.

> *(A short pause.)*

SAM. How do you feel about that?!

AVERY. I mean. She's like…she's like a terrible person.

> That's how I feel about it.

SAM. Have you visited her there?

AVERY. Nope.

SAM. You haven't see your mother for a year and a half?!

AVERY. She came back. A year ago. To visit. When I like…
when a bunch of stuff happened in our family. But I
didn't want to talk to her. I didn't even want to like
look at her.

> *(Pause.)*

SAM. Whoa.

> Whoa.

> *(Pause. They sweep.)*

SAM. For some reason I pictured that you came from a
like perfect family. That like everyone in your family
is super-close and happy and that you all like wear the
same glasses.

AVERY. Uh. No.

> I'm the only one with glasses.

> *(Pause.)*

SAM. You probably should go visit her at some point.

AVERY. I'm not interested.

> *(They sweep for a while. Then **SAM** takes his iPhone out
> of his back pocket and fiddles with it. Then he looks over
> at **AVERY**.)*

SAM. So you wanna see this?

(AVERY nods, then walks over to SAM. SAM holds the phone out in front of AVERY and presses play. We hear the faint noises of the video but cannot make out anything concrete.)

SAM. Okay.

Just…

Keep watching.

It gets funny in like fifteen seconds.

(Fifteen seconds pass. A grin spreads across AVERY's face. SAM starts to giggle.)

SAM. Right?

Ah ha ha ha!

(AVERY nods and grins and maybe silently shakes with a little laughter.)

(The video continues.)

(They watch for a few more seconds and then SAM heaves a satisfied sigh, takes the phone, and puts it back in his pocket.)

(They head to their separate sides of the aisle.)

(ROSE knocks on the window of the projection booth. AVERY looks up. SAM does not. ROSE waves. AVERY waves back and goes back to sweeping. ROSE looks at SAM. She knocks on the window again. SAM does not look up.)

(Blackout.)

Scene Four

(SAM and AVERY sit with their brooms on either side of the aisle. AVERY has a neatly folded letter in his hand that he is about to read out loud.)

SAM. Okay.

Ready.

Actually. Wait.

AVERY. What?

SAM. If I listen to this you have to do Ezekiel 25:17 for me once it's over.

AVERY. Uch. Fine.

SAM. Great. I'm ready.

AVERY. "Dear Mr. Saranac,

My name is Avery Sharpe and I am an employee at the North Brookfield Flick.

I recently learned of your plans to buy the Flick and turn it into the North Brookfield "Venue." I commend you on your keen business sense and your entrepreneurial…" I'm still trying to figure out the right word to use. "Entrepreneurial…"

SAM. Embarkings? Entrepreneurial embarkings?

AVERY. That doesn't make sense.

SAM. Spirit?

AVERY. "I commend you on your keen business sense and your entrepreneurial spirit."

SAM. I like that.

AVERY. I don't know. I just want to be you know, nice/ before I—

SAM. Sure. Sure.

AVERY. I commend you on your etcetera etcetera. Steve Bosco also informed me and the rest of the Flick employees that you intend to keep us on if we so desire and that you—

SAM. Wait. "If we so desire" sounds a little gay.

AVERY. What does that mean?

SAM. It sounds gay.

(in a British accent)

"If we so desire."

AVERY. That's a British accent.

Do you mean it sounds British?

SAM. Same thing.

(Pause.)

AVERY. "—And that you also plan on replacing our 35 millimeter Century projector with a digital projector. I understand you may have many good reasons behind this decision—fewer maintenance fees, simpler training for new projectionists, the unavoidable fact that many movies are now shot digitally, and, of course, the desire to keep working with companies like 20th Century Fox who starting in January will refuse to distribute any of their movies on 35-millimeter film.

(Pause.)

AVERY. *However.*

SAM. Ha-*ha*!

AVERY. However. I urge you to think twice about this decision. You are the only theater in Worcester County, and one of only eight theaters in the entire state of Massachusetts, that still use a film projector. This is an honor, Mr. Saranac. You are carrying a torch and I strongly encourage you not to extinguish it.

SAM. Nice.

AVERY. Movie aficionados like myself come to this theater because of your film projector. And as more and more movie theaters in the United States convert to digital projection I predict that the brave few that continue to use film will become highly valued. You see, Mr. Saranac, the word "film" refers to celluloid. So if you say "Wanna see the new Spielberg film?" you are by definition saying "Wanna see the new Spielberg movie" *on celluloid.* By the way, people like Steven Spielberg have spoken out about this very issue and he is on the record as saying that he will continue to shoot on 35 millimeter until they pry the camera out of his cold, dead hands.

SAM. Wait.

He said that?

AVERY. Well, not the cold dead hands part. That's a /joke.

SAM. Too much. Take it out.

AVERY. Really?

SAM. Yeah. It just makes you sound crazy.

AVERY. Okay. He will continue to shoot on 35 millimeter blahblahblah. Because of people like Mr. Spielberg and many others who WILL continue to shoot on film, it's important that there still be a few remaining theaters that uses film projectors. When you digitally project a movie that was shot on film, you are not actually showing that movie. You are not giving the audience what they paid for.

SAM. Nice. Powerful.

AVERY. Film can express things that computers never will. Film is a series of photographs separated by split seconds of darkness. Film is light and shadow and it is the light and shadow that were there on the day you shot the film.

(*Pause.*)

AVERY. Digital movies—I think the phrase digital film is an oxymoron—are actually just millions of tiny dots. These dots, or pixels, cannot express the variation in color and texture that film can. All the dots are exactly the same size and the same distance apart.

Mr. Saranac, projecting a 35 millimeter film digitally is like looking at a postcard of the Mona Lisa instead of the Mona Lisa itself.

I urge you to keep our beloved Century Projector and to take a stand against the digital takeover of American movies and movie theaters.

Sincerely,

Avery Newton Sharpe.

(Pause.)

SAM. Middle name Newton.

AVERY. Yup. Don't make fun of me.

SAM. I would never.

My middle name is Gruber.

(Pause.)

SAM. I think it's a good letter.

AVERY. You do?

SAM. I do. Something about it is really...

AVERY. What.

SAM. I don't know. It's like something someone would write in a movie. I mean, like the hero of the movie. He'd like bring it to Washington and go like running down the corridor of the courthouse and like stop to kiss the love of his life and she'd say, like, you know, GO FOR IT and then he'd run into the courtroom and read this letter in front of the judge.

AVERY. And what would the judge say?

SAM. You know.

"On this day of all other days..."

"We have learned..."

"I am humbled to admit that even in my old age I can..."

You know:

"This young man has taught us the true meaning of Christmas."

AVERY. Okay. Cool.

(Pause.)

AVERY. Did I convince *you?*

    (Pause.)

SAM. Oh. Hm. Good question.

    (Pause.)

SAM. You know, I guess I don't really care either way.

    (Blackout.)

Scene Five

(The lights in the theater are completely different. It's as if all the bulbs have changed their wattage, or gone fluorescent, or switched location.)

*(**SAM** and **ROSE** are sitting on different sides of the aisle. They are both wearing new uniforms. A yellow polo shirt instead of a maroon one, or vice versa. Now the words "The Venue" are stitched on their pockets.)*

*(**ROSE** and **SAM** are waiting for something. After a silence:)*

SAM. He said I couldn't wear my Red Sox cap anymore.

ROSE. Seriously?

SAM. Uh-huh. And I was like, Paul, we live in Massachusetts. It isn't like a…like a controversial hat.

ROSE. And?

SAM. He didn't go for it.

(After a silence:)

SAM. So how are you?

ROSE. I'm okay.

(Pause.)

ROSE. My roommate left this like long passive-aggressive note on my bedroom door this morning. It was like seven Post-Its long.

And she has this really annoying handwriting.

Anyway, whatever.

(After a pause:)

ROSE. How are *you*? I have no idea how you're /like—

SAM. I'm okay.

(Pause.)

ROSE. What's—what's new?

(Pause.)

SAM. Not much.

    (Pause.)

SAM. I went on a date last night.

ROSE. Oh yeah?

    With like—

    Was it a first date?

SAM. It was a first date.

ROSE. Was it an internet date?

SAM. It was an internet date.

ROSE. And?

SAM. I liked her.

    She was actually pretty cool.

    (Pause.)

SAM. Tiler.

    With an i.

ROSE. Huh.

    (Pause.)

ROSE. What does she do?

SAM. Well.

    At the moment she is a barista—

ROSE. Okay.

SAM. –but she's also sort of a um part-time low-flying trapeze artist.

ROSE. Oh wow.

    (Pause.)

ROSE. So she must have like a really great body.

    (Pause.)

ROSE. If she's like a trapeze artist.

    *(**SAM** sighs. After a short pause:)*

SAM. Why do you have to be so crude?

ROSE. What do/you—

SAM. Like, you're always like, you know, talking about you know, oh, yeah, he had a huge cock, or like, or like, she's like she's like—wow she must have a nice pussy or something.

ROSE. I have never said anything about anyone having a nice pussy in front of you.

SAM. You know. You know what I mean.

ROSE. You must be thinking about Tiler and her nice pussy because I never said/anything about—

SAM. I have been on one date with Tiler!

I have never even kissed Tiler!

(Pause.)

ROSE. Whatever.

SAM. Look, you...you've made it clear that you're not interested. So I don't understand why you can't have a little like you know pity on me and/like—

ROSE. You wouldn't look at me!

SAM. What does—what does—why does—wait—what does that have to do with—why are you—that is like/ completely—

ROSE. You didn't even give me a/chance to—

SAM. You said that I didn't know you! And that...that you were nothing like the person I thought you were! So—

ROSE. So that's true!

(Pause.)

SAM. So—

ROSE. So that's a fact!

(Pause.)

But like...that doesn't mean you have to run out and start like internet dating and like forget all about me.

Like oh yeah, you must be really in love with someone if you like do that.

SAM. So—so—so—so what are you—

Do you like want to go out on a date or something?

(Pause.)

ROSE. No!

SAM. SO WHAT ARE YOU SAYING?!

(Pause.)

ROSE. I'm just saying that I was right. That it was like a… that it was like a big performance.

That's all.

(Pause.)

SAM. I can't believe this.

I can't believe this.

This doesn't make any sense.

(Pause.)

You want me to /like—

ROSE. Just like GET TO KNOW ME!

SAM. I can't get to know you if you keep acting like a…like a…like a…like a—

ROSE. What? Say it.

Say it.

SAM. Never mind.

ROSE. You think I'm like a total bitch.

(Pause.)

ROSE. Right?!

(He doesn't respond.)

ROSE. You like totally hate me now.

So just say it!

*(**AVERY** walks in, also in a new uniform. He looks deeply shaken. They fall silent.)*

AVERY. Hey.

ROSE. How'd it go?

AVERY. Uh—

Well—

SAM. He told *me* I couldn't wear my Red Sox cap anymore.

AVERY. Oh. That sucks.

ROSE. He's got a weird face, right?

(Pause.)

SAM. Did he say anything about your letter?

AVERY. He figured out dinner money.

ROSE. Wait, what?

AVERY. He figured it out.

He looked at the books and looked at the receipts and like—apparently there was like *too* much money in the register from like last month and that's like a sign that people are stealing and then he found the shoebox with the stubs underneath /the—

SAM. Fuck.

Fuck!

ROSE. Wait, why was he looking at the books from last month? What does he care? He has like a whole new system and a credit card machine! We're not gonna steal from *him*!

AVERY. I guess he like…he wanted to make sure we were good employees, or /like—

SAM. So—so what was…

AVERY. He was mad.

(Pause.)

ROSE. Well, yeah. But what /was—

AVERY. And he thinks it's me.

(Pause.)

AVERY. I mean, he thinks it's all me.

(Pause.)

ROSE. Because of your letter?

AVERY. There was a note for Sam in the box. In my handwriting.

(to **SAM***)* From the weekend you were gone.

I guess he recognized my handwriting?

I don't know how he recognized it.

I also think he…

(Pause.)

ROSE. So what did you…

AVERY. I mean, I didn't rat you guys out.

*(**ROSE** and **SAM** both try not to show that they are relieved.)*

SAM. Well.

Okay.

So we just need to uh. To uh.

To uh—

AVERY. Well, I was thinking that you guys could go to him and like fess up to your side of it too and tell him that you were the ones who told me to do it in the first place and /then like—

ROSE. Wait.

What?

AVERY. —and then maybe he won't/like—

ROSE. Waitwaitwaitwaitwait.

Hold on hold on hold on.

Let's all like stop and take a deep breath.

(pause)

Why should we tell him we were the ones who told you to do it in the first place?

(Long pause.)

ROSE. Which by the way is kind of a um whatsitcalled revised way of looking at it. If I recall correctly you were pretty happy to take fifteen bucks from us every night.

AVERY. Because if we say that all of us were doing it and it was like an employee tradition like you said and that everyone did it maybe he'll understand and like...not fire me.

ROSE. He'll fire all of us.

AVERY. I mean, or he'll like let it go.

(Pause.)

ROSE. Whoa.

Okay.

That's really intense.

That's a really intense thing to ask of...to ask us to do.

AVERY. ...I didn't tell on you.

ROSE. Yeah, well, that would have been like *evil*.

(SAM is still silent. They all stand there.)

ROSE. Sam?

SAM. Uh-huh.

ROSE. Do you have anything to say about this?

(He shakes his head no, averting his eyes.)

ROSE. No?

(He shakes his head no again. Both AVERY and ROSE look at him, betrayed.)

ROSE. Okay. Great.

(A horrible, horrible silence.)

ROSE. *(politely, to AVERY)* I'm just um...

How much money does your dad make?

AVERY. Excuse me?

ROSE. I'm just curious. Your dad teaches semantics at Clark, right?

AVERY. Yeah. Semi—

Yeah. I told you that.

ROSE. How much does he make?

AVERY. That's none of your business.

ROSE. And you have a free ride, right?

(Pause.)

AVERY. I don't see how—

ROSE. Because I still have like 20,000 dollars in student loans to pay off and my mom is a secretary.

And I don't have a rich dad.

AVERY. My dad isn't rich.

ROSE. And Sam is 35 and he lives in a shitty attic above his crazy parents.

*(**SAM** winces but does not say anything. Pause.)*

ROSE. And this is our like—this isn't like a job we have *while* we go to college.

This is what we like—feed ourselves with.

(pause)

So I just think that…

AVERY. Wow. Okay.

ROSE. I just think that you should think about that.

(A long pause.)

ROSE. It's just a like really really intense thing to do to ask someone who's super in-debt and someone who didn't even *go* to /college—

SAM. *(quietly)* Okay, Rose—

ROSE. –To like give up their jobs to like defend you.

(Pause.)

ROSE. It just makes me feel like you don't really get it.

*(Pause. **AVERY** just stands there.)*

ROSE. And I mean, I'm really sorry that Paul is blaming you.

That's really fucked up.

*(Another pause. **AVERY** takes off his glasses, polishes them on his shirt, and puts them back on again.)*

(He puts his hands on his hips. He seems to be waiting for something.)

(Finally:)

SAM. What did he say about the projector?

(Pause.)

AVERY. He's getting rid of it.

He's going digital.

(Pause.)

SAM. *(small, hopeful)* So maybe you wouldn't have wanted to stay?

(Pause.)

SAM. *(even more tiny and feeble)* I mean, maybe you would have wanted to quit anyway.

I remember you saying that.

*(**AVERY** looks at **SAM** for a long time, then nods. Then he slowly walks up the aisle towards the door. Then he stops.)*

AVERY. Hey Sam.

*(Pause. **SAM** looks at him.)*

You want me to do Ezekiel 25:17?

SAM. Huh?

AVERY. You want me to do Ezekiel 25:17 for Rose?

(Pause.)

SAM. Uh…maybe…

I'm not sure if now is the right/time to—

AVERY. EZEKIEL 25:17.

THE PATH OF THE RIGHTEOUS MAN IS BESET ON ALL SIDES BY THE INEQUITIES OF THE SELFISH AND THE TYRANNY OF EVIL MEN. BLESSED IS HE WHO, IN THE NAME OF CHARITY AND GOOD WILL, SHEPHERDS THE WEAK THROUGH THE VALLEY OF THE DARKNESS. FOR HE IS TRULY HIS BROTHER'S KEEPER AND THE FINDER OF LOST CHILDREN.

AND I WILL STRIKE DOWN WITH GREAT VENGEANCE AND FURIOUS ANGER THOSE WHO ATTEMPT TO POISON AND DESTROY MY BROTHERS. AND YOU WILL KNOW I AM THE LORD WHEN I LAY MY VENGEANCE UPON YOU.

(Pause. **AVERY** *speaks thoughtfully, sadly.)*

…I been sayin' that shit for years.

And if you ever heard it, it meant your ass.

I never really questioned what it meant. I thought it was just some cold-blooded shit to say to a motherfucker before you popped a cap in his ass.

But I saw some shit this morning that made me think twice.

(after a pause)

Now I'm thinking: it could mean you're the evil man. And I'm the righteous man. And Mr. 9 millimeter here…he's the shepherd protecting my righteous ass in the valley of darkness.

Or it could be, you're the righteous man and I'm the shepherd and it's the world that's evil and selfish. I'd like that.

But that shit ain't the truth.

The truth is, you're the weak.

And I'm the tyranny of evil men.

But I'm tryin', Ringo.

I'm tryin' real hard to be the shepherd.

(He is looking at **SAM**. **SAM** *looks like he might cry. After a silence:)*

ROSE. …That was awesome.

*(***AVERY** *leaves.)*

(Blackout.)

Scene Six

(The theater is dark and empty, The film projector is on. We hear it whirring. Then it flashes green, then white, then goes off.)

(We see **ROSE** *and* **SAM** *enter the projection booth and turn on the lights. They are wearing their new uniforms. They are talking and moving around in the little lit-up window. They seem to be getting along. Maybe at one point* **ROSE** *laughs and hits* **SAM** *on the arm. The theater is still dark.)*

(Then we watch **SAM** *and* **ROSE** *slowly and methodically disassemble the film projector. They remove the reels and then, piece by piece, they remove the film projector from the window and put it on the floor of the projection booth. This might take a little while. Then we watch them install the new digital projector. It doesn't take very long. They turn it on for a second to try it out. It emits a glowing square of white light and then begins to project images. It is on for a while, projecting images we can't see.* **SAM** *and* **ROSE** *leave the booth.)*

(Then the projector goes to green, then white, then darkness. The lights in the movie theater flicker on, and after about five seconds:)

Scene Seven

(The door at the back of the movie theater is thrown open.)

*(**SAM** peeks his head in, looks around, then closes the door.)*

*(A second later, the door opens again and **SAM** drags in a large trash can that he uses to keep the door propped open. Then he exits again and re-enters carrying a large push broom and dustpan.)*

*(**SKYLAR** follows him, carrying a broom of his own.)*

SAM. So this is the walkthrough.

SKYLAR. Cool.

SAM. Pretty easy.

*(**SAM** goes over to his side of the aisle and starts sweeping. **SKYLAR** goes over to the other side of the aisle and starts sweeping. He's a good sweeper. He accidentally kicks a plastic Coke bottle and sends it rolling down the aisle. Then he chases after it, picks it up, and runs it back to the trashcan next to the door. He is speedy. He sweeps faster than **SAM**. **SAM** watches him, impressed.)*

SAM. Have you worked at a movie theater before?

SKYLAR. Yeah. At Cinema World.

In Leominster.

SAM. Oh yeah. I know that one.

(After a pause, trying to make a joke:)

SAM. So you're used to the oversized polo shirt.

SKYLAR. Uh-huh.

(They clean in silence for a while.)

SAM. Did Paul or someone else go over the soda machines with you?

SKYLAR. Yeah. Paul did.

I think I got it.

SAM. Cool.

Cool.

(pause)

Did he talk to you about how to clean the butter dispenser?

SKYLAR. Uh—

SAM. I do Windex and then I use the almond hand soap in the bathroom.

SKYLAR. Oh. Okay.

At my old job we just Windexed and then rinsed it off.

(After a short pause:)

SAM. Yeah.

I would try the almond hand soap too.

SKYLAR. Okay. Cool.

(They keep cleaning.)

SAM. What else.

What else.

(After a pause:)

SAM. For some reason people don't see the garbage can underneath the island...the butter and straws island... it's just...it's like constructed badly. It didn't used to—

Anyway, people think there's no garbage so they like leave all their straw wrappers and stuff on the island so I try to you know swing by there a few times before the movie starts and like brush all the wrappers and like popcorn kernels or whatever into the trash.

SKYLAR. Okay.

(Pause.)

SAM. There used to be three of us working at a time including the projectionist but now it's just two. One of us goes up and presses play when it's time for the movie to start. It's pretty easy.

SKYLAR. Cool.

SAM. If you're working at the same time as Rose you should
    probably let her do it.

SKYLAR. Okay.

   (Pause.)

SAM. We used to…Rose used to like splice together the
    previews.

SKYLAR. Wow.

SAM. Yeah.

   *(They sweep for a while. About twenty seconds of
   sweeping pass. SKYLAR finishes sweeping before SAM. He
   waits patiently in front of the first row. He looks out at
   the movie screen. After a little while, he walks up to the
   movie screen, at the lip of the stage, and then reaches
   out and lightly touches the invisible movie screen. SAM
   notices immediately.)*

SAM. Whoa. What are you doing?

SKYLAR. *(backing away)* Oh. Sorry.

SAM. No. Just—why did you do that?

SKYLAR. …I don't know.

   Sorry.

   (After a pause:)

SKYLAR. I always have this urge to like…

   I always just kind of want to touch it.

   Don't you?

SAM. *(disturbed)* Uh…no.

SKYLAR. Oh. Okay. Sorry.

   *(SKYLAR waits for SAM to finish sweeping. SAM finishes,
   somewhat hurriedly. They head up the aisle. They dump
   their dustbins in the trashcan. They exit. The door slams
   behind them.)*

   (Blackout.)

Scene Eight

(**AVERY**, *in street clothes, is standing in the middle of the aisle, waiting. The door to the theatre is propped open.* **SAM**, *also in street clothes, is up in the projection booth moving around.*)

AVERY. *(calling out)* Are you sure he's not here?

(**SAM** *doesn't hear him. He leaves the booth and a few seconds later he comes down into the hallway with a strange-looking piece of metal equipment. He heaves it onto the floor.*)

AVERY. Are you sure he isn't gonna like come in all of a sudden?

SAM. Yeah, yeah. He's away for the weekend.

Trust me.

(**SAM** *disappears again. A few seconds later we see him in the booth, moving around. He leaves and then comes down with another piece of equipment. He puts it down in the hallway next to the first piece.*)

AVERY. He's not gonna notice it's gone?

SAM. He tried to sell it on eBay and nobody wanted it. So he told me to donate it as scrap metal.

I've been saving it for you.

(**SAM** *disappears again.* **AVERY** *waits. He looks at the movie screen for a little while. Then* **AVERY** *walks into the hallway, picks up the first piece of equipment, and leaves. A few seconds later,* **SAM** *comes down again with another piece of equipment. It's becoming clear that he is bringing down pieces of the dissembled film projector. He looks around for* **AVERY**, *confused. A few seconds later,* **AVERY** *returns.*)

SAM. Where'd you go?

AVERY. My dad is waiting out front. In his car.

SAM. Oh. Okay.

(*SAM disappears again.* AVERY *picks up two pieces and disappears again.* SAM *comes down again with the last piece of the projector. A few seconds later,* AVERY *comes in again, wiping his hands on his pants.*)

SAM. This is it.

AVERY. Okay. Cool.

(*They stand there for a second.*)

SAM. Oh. Wait.

(*SAM runs back up to the projection booth. We see him grab two octagonal cases. He comes back down with them.* AVERY *has wandered into the aisle of the theater.*)

SAM. Some of Steve's old reels. He took most of the good ones. But there are a couple left.

AVERY. Oh. Okay.

(*SAM puts each one down on the floor, reading its label out loud while he does this.*)

SAM. *Crouching Tiger Hidden Dragon…*

Rugrats in Paris…

(*He runs back up to the booth, then comes back down with two more cases, heaving them down on the ground.*)

SAM. *Star Trek Insurrection…*

…and *Honey I Shrunk The Kids.*

That's actually a pretty good find.

You want them?

We were just gonna throw these out too.

AVERY. Um.

Yeah. Sure.

Hold on.

(*He picks up two cases, leaves the theater, and then returns 30 seconds later. He picks up the last two cases and holds them, one in each hand. They are heavy.*)

SAM. So what are you gonna do with the projector?

AVERY. I don't know. Start some kind of underground basement cinema movement?

(SAM laughs.)

AVERY. I'm sort of serious.

SAM. Oh. Okay. Cool.

AVERY. Maybe when I go back to Clark in the fall I'll form a 35 millimeter film society. I don't know.

Own my own theater some day.

SAM. Awesome.

(A long pause.)

SAM. Look.

I uh—

(Another pause. Maybe AVERY has to put down a case because it is too heavy.)

SAM. I'm sorry, Avery.

(A pause.)

AVERY. No. I mean. Whatever. It was good for me.

(A pause.)

AVERY. I had some kind of stupid idea that we were friends./And then—

SAM. *(in pain)* Oh god.

AVERY. Let me finish. And then it became like very clear that we…

Look, everything that's…everything that's like ever happened to me has disappointed me. The world keeps…

So clearly I'm like…clearly I'm like putting too much faith in stuff.

(Pause.)

I mean, I think the truth is that you can't trust anybody.

SAM. That's not true.

AVERY. No, I don't mean that in a bad way. Not like everyone is untrustworthy or something. Just like, don't expect anything. Don't expect things to turn out well in the end.

SAM. Uh...I don't know if I agree with that world view.

AVERY. Look, realizing that has helped me.

It's actually made me feel okay for the first time in a while. I like let go of...

(Pause.)

AVERY. I'm not saying I want to be friends with you or anything. I don't.

(after a short pause)

And you know, we were never really friends in the first place. I let Rose show me how to use the projector.

Every man for himself, you know?

SAM. Jesus, Avery.

AVERY. I think that's the way it goes.

(unable to help himself)

And the truth is, one day I'll come back to visit Massachusetts and you'll still be here sweeping up popcorn. Working for some bigot from Nashua. And I'll be like...I'll be living in Paris or something. So... you know.

(Pause.)

AVERY. Thanks for thinking of me. And for saving the projector. And the film.

(Pause. AVERY bends down and picks up the last case.)

AVERY. Do you remember the end of the movie *Manhattan*?

SAM. Uh—

AVERY. Woody Allen like realizes he's still in love with Mariel Hemingway and he like runs down the street and finds her in her doorway and she's getting ready to go to London and she's brushing her hair and he's like stay here with me or whatever, and she's like, no, I'm leaving, and he's like, but what's gonna happen? and she's like:

"You gotta have a little faith in people" and the music swells up?

SAM. Oh.

Yeah.

AVERY. This is like the opposite of that ending.

(**AVERY** *turns to go and starts walking up the aisle towards the door.*)

SAM. Look. Avery. Just—before you go. I know my life might seem kind of depressing to you, and you know, in a lot of ways it is.

But there's some good stuff in it.

Maybe I never told you about it, but there's some really good stuff in my life.

(*Pause.*)

SAM. And sometimes the people you fall in love with fall in love with you back.

(*Pause.*)

SAM. Sometimes they don't. But sometimes they do. And it's awesome.

(*Pause.*)

SAM. And I feel like once that happens to /you—

AVERY. Okay. Thanks for the advice, Sam.

(**AVERY** *walks towards the door. As he exits:*)

SAM. Macaulay Culkin to Michael Caine.

(**AVERY** *stops and shakes his head no.*)

SAM. Macaulay Culkin to Michael Caine.

AVERY. See ya, Sam.

(*AVERY walks out the door. It shuts behind him.* **SAM**
*stands in the aisle of the movie theater, his hands stuffed
in the pockets of his pants. He stares at the door, waiting.
A very very long amount of time passes.*)

(*Maybe a minute and a half.*)

(**SAM** *stands there patiently.*)

(*Suddenly* **AVERY** *comes back in through the doors,
unsmiling.*)

AVERY. Macaulay Culkin to Mandy Moore in *Saved.*

(**SAM** *bursts into a beatific grin.*)

AVERY. Mandy Moore to Robin Williams in *License to Wed.*

Robin Williams to Jude Law in *A.I.*

SAM. Robin Williams was /in—?

AVERY. I think it was uncredited.

He was like the voice of the computer robot guy.

Trust me.

SAM. Okay.

AVERY. …Jude Law to Michael Caine in *Sleuth.*

(*They look at each other.* **AVERY** *is still unsmiling.*)

AVERY. Easy.

(*And with that,* **AVERY** *leaves. The doors shut behind
him.* **SAM** *sits down in one of the seats, smiling to
himself.*)

(*One of the orchestral themes from "Jules and Jim"
["Vacances" by Georges Delerue]* starts playing,
underscoring* **SAM**'s *movements.*)

(**SAM** *puts his feet up on the seat in front of him and
looks up at the ceiling of the movie theater for a while.
Then he gets up, still smiling, and walks up the aisle.*

---

*Please see Music Use Note on page 3

Right before he exits, he flicks off the lights. The theater is plunged into darkness. The sound of the door closing.)

(The music swells.)

(Blackout.)

End of Play